CODED TRUTHS

THE BILLIONAIRES OF CREST STRATEGIES
BOOK 4

ELORA RAE

ALSO BY ELORA RAE

The Billionaires Of Crest Strategies

To everyone who fell for the nerd and wants to see him shine in the dark romance spotlight.

TRIGGER/CONTENT WARNING

Hey gorgeous (likely unhinged) readers!

This novella is a dark billionaire romance.

Before you dive into Penn and Victoria's obsessively romantic love story, let's chat about what you're getting into because we all know that in this genre, content warnings are how we choose books...

Inside this book, you'll find:
- **Stalking and surveillance**: Extensive monitoring including hidden cameras in the heroine's apartment, tracking of daily routines, and four years of secret observation
- **Childhood trauma and suicide**: Depiction of a teenage suicide attempt, including the moments leading up to it and the intervention (handled with care but present in backstory)
- **Violence and blood**: Including armed attacks, kidnapping, physical torture, beatings, gunshot wounds, and murder
- **Witness protection and family trauma**: Parental murder (assassination), forced identity changes, and ongoing threats to family members

- **Child endangerment**: A teenage girl is kidnapped, held captive, and threatened (she survives but experiences trauma). It is insinuated that she experienced SA while abducted, so please read with caution
- **Excessive swearing and profanity**: These characters have filthy mouths in more ways than one
- **Spicy, high-heat sex scenes**: Including sex during high-stress situations, oral sex, sex toys, anal play, spanking, and bondage (all consensual)

Other content warnings: Neurodivergent representation (ADHD and autism spectrum), bullying (past), panic attacks and PTSD responses, implied sexual assault of a minor (does not happen on page, perpetrator is dealt with), police corruption and betrayal, systemic witness elimination, life-threatening injuries, and characters in mortal danger.

I did say it was dark...

The good news? The stalking becomes consensual protection. Penn's surveillance is obsessive but not malicious. The relationship develops into mutual devotion with healthy communication established by the end. The darkness comes from external threats and past trauma, not from toxic dynamics between Penn and Victoria.

If any of these themes are upsetting or not your thing, please take care while reading, or maybe skip this one. There are lots of amazing books out there, so find the ones that bring you joy, not stress.

But if you're here for a tense, sexy, high-stakes story where a neurodivergent billionaire tech genius has been obsessively protecting his mysteriously-disappeared high school sweetheart whether she knows it or not...

Welcome to the *Billionaires of Crest Strategies*.

You've been warned.

Happy reading!

-Elora

P.S. If you or someone you know is struggling with thoughts of suicide, please reach out for help. Like the characters in this book, you are not alone, and there are people who want to support you.

National Suicide Prevention Lifeline (US): *988 (call or text)*

Crisis Text Line: *Text HOME to 741741*

International Association for Suicide Prevention: *https://www.iasp.info/resources/Crisis_Centres/*

If you're in crisis, please prioritize your wellbeing and seek support. The right help can make all the difference.

CHAPTER ONE

VICTORIA

THE CURTAIN ROSE ON THE MASQUERADE SCENE, AND Victoria melted into Meg Giry's posture—back straight, hands clasped, the perfect obedient ballet rat. The stage lights hit her like a baptism, burning away everything that wasn't this moment, this role. She could vanish here. No past, no future, just the rush of the orchestra and the electric hum of an audience holding its breath.

The sopranos hit their high notes, and Victoria spun into the choreography—feet precise, skirts whispering against her thighs. The Phantom's shadow loomed on the layered set behind her, but she didn't flinch. Stagecraft. Fake chandeliers, fake danger. Nothing like the real thing.

A collective gasp rippled through the crowd as the Phantom's noose snapped tight around Buquet's neck. Victoria let her own breath hitch—Meg was supposed to be afraid, and god, it felt good to let fear be pretend. When stagehands yanked the prop body into the flies, she let a tremor run through her arms. Someone in the wings murmured, "Damn, Omstadt sells it every night."

Easy when you've practiced.

She pirouetted into the next formation, sweat prickling at her temples under the wig. The spotlight found her. Not her, though. Meg. She was Meg.

When the final curtain fell to thunderous applause, Victoria held her pose—Meg's wide-eyed innocence—until the houselights killed the magic. The illusion shattered. Shoulders dropping, she peeled off the character like a second skin as the cast dissolved into chatter and sweaty hugs around her.

Backstage smelled of rosin and hairspray, the air thick with the collective exhalation of twenty performers shedding their roles. Victoria navigated the maze of props and cables with muscle memory, her body still humming with leftover adrenaline. For three hours, she hadn't been the girl with the clenched jaw in grocery store lines, or the woman who triple-checked her door locks. She'd been Meg— sweet, uncomplicated Meg.

The collective dressing room was a sanctuary of cracked mirrors and wilting bouquets from well-wishers. Tonight, a new arrangement sat atop her vanity: white peonies wrapped in brown paper, their petals trembling when she shut the door behind her. No ribbon, no card—just a slip of paper tucked between the stems.

"Your Meg makes them
forget Christine exists."

Victoria's fingers hovered over the note. Eleven performances just this month, eleven bouquets. Always peonies. Always unsigned. It'd been that way since her very first show four years ago.

A giggle burst out of her. Backlit by the vanity bulbs, the flowers glowed like stage lights. The Phantom sent Christine roses; her phantom sent peonies.

She tucked the note into her script and reached for the cold cream. In the mirror, her reflection flickered between gratitude and unease. Gifts meant attention. Attention meant being seen.

But for the length of the overture, the length of an aria, she wanted to be seen, even if she had to go back to invisibility afterwards.

The peonies trembled as she wiped away Meg's blush. The dressing room door banged open, releasing a burst of laughter and the smell of perfume. Christine flounced in, her silk robe gaping as she shoved sweaty dark curls off her forehead. "Queen Meg strikes again! Bet they're giving you my role next season." She grinned, ripping off her petticoat like a bandage.

Victoria chuckled, massaging cold cream into her cheeks. "Wouldn't that be a twist?" The familiar script of backstage banter had her grinning. "But you can keep Christine. I love Meg."

"And she loves you, V." Madame Giry swept in next, still stiff-backed even as she peeled off her gloves. "Your footwork during the ballet was immaculate tonight." She squeezed Victoria's shoulder as she passed to her own vanity.

Other chorus girls trailed in behind her, chattering about post-show drinks. One elbowed Victoria's shoulder. "Coming tonight?"

"Raincheck," Victoria said, snapping her makeup case shut.

"Oh, you're no fun." The flock of them dispersed in a flutter of wet wipes and costume bags.

Victoria pulled off the wig cap, shaking out her real hair—a deep auburn this month—then scrubbed until her skin burned pink. In the mirror, Victoria Omstadt emerged inch by inch until Meg was just a smudge of glitter under her nails. She changed into her oversized hoodie and sweatpants, lacing her tennis shoes tightly.

The backstage lights dimmed as the last of the cast trickled out, their laughter echoing down the hall until it dissolved into silence. Victoria lingered, the only sound being the soft creak of her chair as she leaned back. Her fingers traced the edge of the vanity, where the peonies sat, their white petals stark against the cluttered surface. Her reflection stared back with tired green eyes. She looked like herself now, whoever that was.

The note still tucked in her script stared up at her. She pulled it out, smoothing the creases with her thumb. The handwriting was so neat it almost looked printed. Maybe it was. She'd spent a few days the first time the flowers arrived four years ago trying to figure out who had sent them, but gave up when she found nothing. It had unsettled her at first. All the others received flowers from friends, family, and fans. It was normal. But for her, because of her past, it had felt…threatening. But they kept coming, and not once had the person revealed themselves. Four years of performances nearly every night, flowers, every night.

Whoever was sending them had money to burn, it seemed.

Victoria folded the note and slipped it into her bag, standing to grab her coat. With another glance around the room to make sure she'd picked up all of her belongings, Victoria flipped the light switch and left out the side door.

The alley behind the theater was a canyon of brick and shadow. She hated it every night. Her sneakers scuffed against the pavement, the sound swallowed by the city's hum. She pulled her hood up, her breath visible in the cold. The streets were quieter now, but not empty. A cab hissed past, its headlights cutting through the dark. Victoria's fingers tightened around her keys, one poking awkwardly between her knuckles. The streetlights buzzed overhead, throwing long shadows that stretched too far—like someone could step out of them at any second. Baby hairs on the nape of her neck prickled.

She glanced back. Nothing. Just the usual graffiti-scarred walls and the distant laughter of strangers spilling out of a bar. But the feeling clung anyway, sticky as sweat.

Victoria quickened her pace.

Twenty steps later, the air shifted behind her. A scrape of a shoe she hadn't seen coming. She whipped around.

Empty sidewalk.

Her pulse thrummed. Could've sworn—

No. Nothing.

The fluorescent glow of a bodega flickered ahead like a beacon. She crossed the street without checking for traffic (there was never traffic at this hour, but she always checked—always—except tonight, when her body was already moving before logic kicked in). The door chimed as she shoved inside.

"Evening," the clerk mumbled without looking up from his phone.

Victoria grabbed the first thing her fingers touched—spearmint gum—and slapped it onto the counter. Her reflection in the security camera footage looked warped.

She forced her fingers still as she fished out a crumpled bill.

"That all?" The clerk asked, still not looking up from his phone.

Victoria pressed her lips together and pocketed the gum she didn't want. "Yeah. Thanks."

The bell jingled again as she stepped back into the dark.

Her apartment was three blocks away. Three. She exhaled through her nose and started walking; fast enough she wouldn't have to hear footsteps behind her, slow enough she wouldn't look like she was running.

A shadow moved where it shouldn't. Across the street. Between parked cars. Victoria froze.

The streetlamp caught pale fingers retreating into the dark. The glimpse vanished so fast she couldn't be sure she'd seen it at all. But she had. She knew she had.

Her reflection flickered in a shop window as she passed; her face pale, her shoulders tense. The shadow behind her was just a blur, but it was there. She ducked into a narrow side street, her heart pounding. The footsteps paused. Then they stopped.

Victoria held her breath, pressing herself against the wall. When she finally dared to peek around the corner, the street was empty. Just the glow of a streetlamp and the distant rumble of the subway.

She exhaled, her breath shaky. Victoria forced herself to keep moving, her pace steady now, her keys still clenched in her fist. The city loomed around her, its windows like unblinking eyes. She didn't look back.

The security gate to her apartment building screeched shut behind her, the metallic clang loud enough to make Victoria flinch. She pressed her palm against the door until she heard the lock click, her shoulders finally dropping a fraction. The lobby smelled of stale takeout and lemon floor cleaner, the flickering lights buzzing like an angry fly. Up the stairwell she went—always the stairs, never the elevator—her tennis shoes silent against the chipped concrete steps.

By the fourth floor, her calves complained, but the ache was welcome. She fumbled with her keys outside 4C. Inside, nails scrambled against hardwood.

"Hey, baby." She crouched as Sandy barreled into her, tail thumping, wet nose pressing into her collarbone. The dog's whole body wriggled—too big to be a lapdog, too small to be intimidating, but her warmth seeped into Victoria's bones like sunshine. She buried her face in Sandy's golden fur, inhaling the familiar scent of dog shampoo and the faint musk of home. "Missed you too, girly."

Victoria shrugged off her bag, letting it slump onto the armchair. The peonies went into a chipped vase on the kitchen counter, their petals already unfurling in the warmth. Her fingers lingered on the stems as she plucked the old bouquet—slightly wilted, edges browning—and dumped it into the trash. Every surface held flowers: a bouquet on the bookshelf, another on the nightstand, and yet another near the bathroom sink. All from him. Her phantom.

After she closed the blinds and the curtains for good measure, Victoria checked the door was locked and started getting comfortable. Peeling off her sweatshirt and bra with a sigh, Victoria traded them for an oversized NYU T-shirt that swallowed her frame. The sweatpants followed, kicked carelessly toward the laundry basket. Cool air kissed her bare thighs as she padded across to her kitchenette. The studio apartment wasn't large, but she'd made it Sandy and her home.

Popcorn rattled in the microwave, kernels bursting one by one. She poured herself a generous glass of red—the cheap kind that came in a large box—and curled onto the bed. Sandy flopped beside her, immediately commandeering half the pillows.

"Annie, 1982," Victoria told the screen as she queued it up. The opening credits blared, and Sandy perked up at the familiar tune, tail thumping against the comforter. Victoria grinned, scratching behind her ears. "Yeah, yeah, I know. Your namesake."

Halfway through "Maybe," her phone buzzed. Clara's face flashed on screen—her sister's freckled nose scrunched in a smirk, braces glinting. Victoria swiped to answer.

"You watching it too?" Clara's voice crackled through the speaker.

On her tiny screen, TV light flickered across Clara's face, the same opening scene playing behind her.

Victoria held up her bowl of popcorn in salute. "Obviously."

Clara rolled her eyes but snuggled deeper into her blanket cocoon. "You're so predictable."

"Says the person also watching it." Victoria took a slow sip of wine, studying her sister's face—the dark circles under her eyes, the way her fingers picked at her cuticles. "Rough week?"

Clara hesitated, then shrugged. "Geometry test. Ms. Gerard's a killer."

Victoria frowned. "You studied, though. You'll crush it."

"I dunno. I blanked on the practice exam."

"Hey." Victoria waited until Clara met her gaze through the screen. "You're smarter than you think. And if Gerard fails you, I'll make her disappear."

Clara snorted. "You'd get caught in, like, five minutes."

"Three, max."

Laughter burst out of Clara, and Victoria's chest warmed. They settled back into the movie, occasionally mouthing along to lines in unison. Comfort in the shared ritual.

"I should get to bed," Clara mumbled when the credits rolled, already half-asleep.

"Text me after the test," Victoria whispered. "And no caffeine past eight, or you'll be wired."

"Yes, *Mom*."

The call ended, leaving the apartment too quiet. Victoria set the phone aside and stared at the blackened screen. Sandy whined, nosing her elbow.

"Okay, okay." Victoria scratched behind her ears again, but her gaze drifted to the window. The blinds were shut tight. No gaps. No shadows. And even if there were, her curtains were a second set of protection.

So why did she still feel watched?

CHAPTER TWO

PENN

Sixteen monitors glowed in the dark of Penn Levine's tech sanctuary, their blue light reflecting off the reinforced glass walls of his control room. Penn loosened his bow tie but didn't take it off. He never did. Just like he never deviated from the routine: black suit, white shirt, no cufflinks (they clicked against keyboards), shoes polished to a high shine but scuffed at the heels because he paced when he got anxious. And shit. He was anxious.

Victoria was home now and hadn't noticed the man with the gun.

How had she not noticed the man with the gun?

He had a fucking gun.

Penn tapped the desktop, switching camera feeds—her building's exterior, the alley, then back to the grainy footage of the dark-clad figure who had turned the corner just as she reached her stoop. The feed rewound, paused, sharpened. No clear facial signature. No visible tattoos. A side-holstered weapon, though—Blackhawk Serpa. Professional.

His fingers drummed against the mechanical keyboard. Drummed again. Faster now. Penn pushed his blue-light filtering glasses higher on his nose.

Victoria appeared on the central screen, bare-legged in that damn

NYU shirt, pouring wine into a mug. Her dog, Sandy, pressed against her thigh, and Penn caught the way Victoria's breath audibly slowed when she touched the dog.

He scrubbed a hand through his short hair, messing up the careful styling his stylist had forced on him before the gala he'd attended earlier. (He skipped most of it. Escaped to the theater instead, watching Victoria play Meg Giry as she had since she'd landed the role. Penn had sat in his normal seat, having bought out the box for the entire month, counting each rotation to make sure none of the other dancers got too close. None ever did.)

Four years of white peonies. Four years of silent surveillance. Four years of watching Victoria Omstadt without ever crossing the razor-thin line between observation and contact. He wasn't supposed to have this footage—wasn't supposed to have hacked the theater's security cams, the traffic feeds, the smart lock on her apartment door. But where rules existed, Penn bypassed them.

Onscreen, Victoria sprawled on her bed, laughing at something her sister said over a video call. The sound quality was good—he'd calibrated the mic himself. If he really wanted, he could pull up the call on one of the screens and get an even clearer audio feed, but there was no need. It was just her sister.

Another monitor pinged. The facial recognition software still churned through databases, cross-referencing the blurry image of the man who had followed her. No results. Not yet.

Penn's jaw tightened.

The man had a fucking gun, and he was following Victoria.

Pulling up another program, Penn's fingers flew across three separate keyboards—Crest Systems' encrypted server, then Tanner's contact. The line rang twice before Tanner's wife answered.

"Penn," Blair said, and Penn could hear the smile in her voice. "Tanner's not here right now. What do you need?"

Penn exhaled through his nose. He should have texted. Talking was inefficient. "Tell him—" His fingers flexed. "Tell him I have a security situation. Not urgent yet. I'll text him details tomorrow."

A pause. When she spoke again, her voice was softer. "Are you okay?"

His thumb tapped the spacebar—once, twice—cycling the cameras back to Victoria's living room. Empty wine glass. Old movie credits. Sandy snoring. Safe. For now.

"I'm fine. Thanks, Blair."

"Of course. I'll let him know," Blair said, and the call ended.

Penn set the phone down and bit his lip. With another look at the image of Victoria lying on her bed, Penn reached for the fidget spinner he'd had made out of tungsten and a full ceramic bearing. It spun around and around as he watched.

And watched.

Just like every night.

———

THE LAB BUZZED WITH THE HUM OF MACHINERY AND THE rhythmic clack of Penn's fingers across keyboards. His glasses slipped down his nose, and he pushed them back up with a knuckle, his other hand shoving a handful of chips into his mouth. He hadn't slept, hadn't moved from his chair except to grab more caffeine from the fridge. His bow tie was gone, his shirt untucked with the sleeves rolled up, and his jacket hung limply over the back of his chair. A cluster of energy drink cans littered the desk.

The security feed on the center monitor replayed the man in the alley—the same man, the same gun, the same deliberate shadow that trailed Victoria home. Penn ground his teeth every time he saw it. He'd need to visit his dentist later that day at this rate. The facial recognition software was still running, but had spat out nothing. Whoever this guy was, he was too good at staying invisible.

The intercom buzzed, and Penn's hand shot to the control panel, pulling up the exterior camera feed. Tanner stood at the door, his 6-foot-6 frame filling the screen.

"Gonna let me in, asshat?" Tanner's voice came through the radio garbled.

"Yeah, one sec." Penn hit the release button without hesitation. "Tanner," he muttered to himself, straightening his shirt halfheartedly. "Right. Tanner."

By the time Tanner reached the control room, Penn was back at his desk, spinning the tungsten fidget spinner between his fingers. Tanner's sharp eyes took in the chaos—the monitors, the empty cans, Penn's disheveled state.

"You look like fucking hell, man," Tanner said, his arms crossing over his chest like some twisted version of a scolding mother hen.

Penn didn't look up, glancing at his friend's reflection in one of the monitors. "I'm fine."

"Blair said you had a security situation."

"I do." Penn pulled up the footage of the man in the alley. Tanner leaned in, his brow furrowing as he studied the grainy image.

"Who is he?"

"Don't know yet. He followed someone home last night."

"Someone?"

"Yeah. She...she's an actress." Penn hesitated, his thumb tapping the edge of the fidget spinner. "Victoria Omstadt."

Tanner straightened, his gaze narrowing. "Why are we worried about an actress?"

Penn's fingers froze on the spinner. "I've been watching her."

"Watching her." Tanner's tone was flat, but the unspoken accusation hung in the air.

"For four years," Penn admitted, his voice tight.

Tanner crossed his arms. "Four years. You've been stalking this woman for four fucking years."

Penn's jaw clenched. Yeah, he really needed to see his dentist because that fucking hurt. "It's not stalking. It's... protective surveillance."

"Semantics. Why?"

Penn's throat felt dry. He reached for a can of energy drink, cracked it open, and took a long sip, buying himself a moment. His internal thoughts clashed. How much could he say? How much *should* he say?

"She's... important," he finally said.

11

Tanner raised an eyebrow. "Important how?"

Penn avoided the question. "She used to have a different name. I'm doing a favor for a friend."

It wasn't a lie. Not entirely. The memory of Vanessa—her green eyes, her voice—flashed in his mind. She had saved him when he was a kid. She'd been the only person who'd ever seen him—really seen him. And then she'd disappeared.

Tanner exhaled sharply. "Penn, you know I have your back for almost anything, but Crest Strategies is a reputation rehabilitation company, not a security firm. If she's in danger, call the cops."

"You think I haven't thought of that?" Penn spun his chair around to face Tanner fully. "I realize this isn't what we usually do, but damn it, Tanner, you helped Carson when he all but stalked Kinsley and got her kidnapped. And when Paisley went missing, you helped then too. I'm just trying to be proactive before this woman goes missing. You and Jenna handle security, and I need your help."

"Yeah, well, Cars and Ben were in love with those women when I helped."

"So you're admitting you were a fucking teddy bear before Blair?"

"Is this your way of asking for help? Insulting me?" Tanner's expression didn't soften. "Look, man, this isn't what we do. Those were one off experiences. At least I fucking hope so."

"But this could be what we do," Penn shot back. "We have the resources. The skills. And she's in danger."

"And she's also a stranger."

"Not to me."

"Stalking the poor girl for four fucking years doesn't mean you know her. It means you're a little too good with tech." Tanner studied him for a long moment, then sighed. "Fine. If this is as serious as you say, you need to bring it to the team. The *whole* team. Not just me and not just Briggs. You need to bring this to Carson, Benedict, James. All of us."

Penn's stomach twisted. Presenting this to the team meant exposure, meant questions he wasn't ready to answer. But the image of the man with the gun burned in his mind.

"Will you support me if I do?"

Tanner ran a hand through his short hair. "I guess, though I don't condone stalking."

"But you condone cutting off a man's fingers and stabbing him in the eyeball?"

"Levine," Tanner growled out Penn's last name in a warning.

"Fine," Penn sighed. "I'll present it."

————

THE CREST STRATEGIES CONFERENCE ROOM WAS TOO FULL. Or maybe it was just nerves. Penn stood at the head of the table, his jacket on, but his hair still stubbornly stuck up in a few spots. He had cleaned up as much as he could in the twenty minutes since Tanner had left.

Carson Crest sat at the opposite end of the table, his steel-gray eyes sharp as ever as they fixed on Penn. Benedict Astor leaned back in his chair, his attention on his tablet. James Rothschild sat to his left, expressionless, though his gaze occasionally flicked to Jenna Briggs, their head of security, where she leaned against the wall, her arms crossed. Tanner stood beside her, his towering presence making even the large room feel smaller.

"Penn," Carson said, breaking the silence. "You said you have something to present."

Penn nodded, his throat dry. God, he needed an energy drink. And his fidget spinner. And about a gallon of liquid courage. He hit a button on the remote in his hand, and the wall screens lit up with the security footage of the man in the alley.

"This man followed a woman by the name of Victoria Omstadt home last night," Penn began, his voice steady despite the unease churning in his gut. "He's armed, professional, and I haven't been able to identify him."

Carson's eyes narrowed. "And why are we worried about this woman?"

Penn hesitated, his thumb tracing the edge of the remote. "She's... connected to someone I used to know. Someone who's important."

Across the table, Carson leaned forward, his brow rising in a skeptical look. "Details."

Penn's fingers tightened around the remote. "She..." He cleared his throat. "We knew each other. Years ago. Before Broadway."

Benedict adjusted his glasses. "Define 'knew.'"

"Not like that." The words came out too fast. "Just—a long time ago. And then four years back, when she was just starting out, I found her again."

Carson didn't blink. "And?"

Shifting on his feet, Penn pushed his glasses up his nose. "I... kept tabs on her."

"What, like... security checks?" Jenna asked.

"Sure."

"Penn." Benedict's voice was calm. "Give us specifics."

His pulse thudded in his ears. He couldn't bring himself to look at them, so he focused on the screen instead. "I went to her shows. All of them. Tapped into street cams near her apartment. Tracked her phone location—just GPS, no content. Well, sometimes the content." He hesitated. "And I set up alerts for her name in news outlets, social media."

Tanner let out a low whistle. "Jesus."

Penn's jaw clenched. "It wasn't—"

"Stalking." James stated it flatly. "You're describing stalking."

Penn shot a glance at Carson. "Well, you watched Kinsley for years before you even got her on as a client."

Carson's expression didn't change, but his knuckles whitened slightly where his hands rested on the tabletop. "That was different."

"How?"

"It was strategic."

"My reasons weren't?" Penn couldn't stop the edge in his voice. "I want to keep her safe. I—" He stopped himself before admitting to the camera in her apartment.

Jenna pushed off the wall. "Here's the problem. You don't even realize how creepy this sounds."

"It wasn't—"

"I don't care if you think you had reasons." Jenna crossed her arms. "You made yourself her silent shadow for four years. That's not protection, it's obsession."

Penn's face burned. He opened his mouth, but Tanner cut in.

"Look," Tanner rumbled, arms folded. "Does it make me uncomfortable? Yeah. But we've all crossed lines when someone we care about is involved." He shot a pointed look at Carson. "And if there's a genuine threat, we deal with it first. Morals later."

Carson exhaled sharply through his nose, then turned to Jenna. "Can you spare anyone to watch her?"

Jenna hesitated, then nodded. "I can pull a few from the lower-tier ops. But—"

"But," Carson said smoothly, "Penn has to tell her."

Penn's stomach dropped. "What?"

"You tell Ms. Omstadt," Carson repeated. "About the surveillance. No more secrets. If she walks away, you let her."

Penn's breath hitched. "You can't be serious." His fingers twitched around the remote, a screensaver of Victoria walking her dog flickering behind him.

Carson didn't blink. "You tell her. Or this isn't Crest business."

"No—that's—" Penn's pulse hammered in his skull. He shot a desperate look at Tanner, who only lifted his big shoulders in a shrug.

"Sorry man, but you dug this hole," Tanner said.

She'll hate you, hissed the voice in his head. *She'll run. She'll call the cops. All those years of watching her, and you never once—*

Benedict cleared his throat. "We know you're coming from a good place, Penn. But the fact remains that we can't offer her protection without her agreeing to it."

"Especially legally," James added.

Jenna's arms were still crossed. "She deserves to know. Anything less makes us the stalkers too."

Penn's throat tightened. He stared at the remote in his hand, the weight of it suddenly unbearable. If he told her, Victoria would look at him the way Jenna just had—with disgust, with fear. He'd memorized the warmth in her laugh from four rows back at the theater, the way she absentmindedly tucked her hair behind her ear when reading scripts. All of it would vanish the second she realized he'd been watching.

His fingers twitched. He could walk away. Just drop it. But the image of that man—shoulders squared, hand near his holster—flashed behind his eyes. Professionals didn't follow someone like that without reason.

Carson adjusted his cuff links. "Well?"

Penn swallowed hard. It was her or the threat. "Fine," he muttered, the word scraping out. "I'll tell her."

Carson stood abruptly. "Then we're done."

Jenna moved for the door, Tanner behind her. Benedict lingered just long enough to give Penn an unreadable look before following. James stayed. For a long moment, neither spoke.

"Cameras?" James asked quietly.

Penn stiffened. James didn't press. Just nodded once, like he already knew. Then he left too. Alone, Penn sank into a chair and dragged a hand over his face. He had to tell her.

And she was going to hate him.

CHAPTER THREE

VICTORIA

Victoria adjusted the strap of her bag, the crinkle of cellophane from her latest bouquet of peonies brushing against her hip with each step. The night air curled in around her as she rolled her shoulders back, trying to shake off the lingering tension from the performance. Tonight's show had been brilliant.

But the familiar prickle at the nape of her neck wouldn't fade.

She glanced over her shoulder. The sidewalk behind her was empty except for a lone figure in a dark hoodie half a block back, hands shoved in his pockets. Nothing unusual. Nothing threatening.

You're being paranoid.

She forced a slow breath through her nose. Ahead, the glow of her apartment building's awning beckoned. Just a few more blocks. She could already picture the shower waiting for her, the way the hot water would loosen the last of the stage makeup from her skin. Sandy would be curled on the bed, ears perking the second she turned the key in the lock.

A footstep scuffed too close behind her.

Her pulse jumped. She didn't turn. Just picked up her pace, fingers tightening around her keys, the jagged teeth pressing into her palm.

Almost home.

A hand clamped over her mouth.

She barely had time to gasp before an arm locked around her waist, yanking her backward into the alley's yawning darkness. The peonies tumbled from her bag, petals scattering across the pavement. Her elbow jerked back, aiming for ribs, but her attacker twisted, slamming her against the brick wall. The impact knocked the breath out of her lungs.

A mask. Black fabric stretched over the lower half of his face, eyes shadowed under the hood.

"Don't scream," he hissed.

Her knee came up—instinct, training—but he blocked it with his thigh, pinning her harder against the wall. His free hand flicked open a switchblade, the steel catching the dim glow of a distant streetlight.

Victoria bucked hard, twisting against the masked man's grip. The rough brick scraped her shoulders as she tried to knee him again, but he pressed in tighter, the knife flashing near her face. Her pulse hammered so loudly in her ears she barely heard his next words.

"Easy, Vanessa."

Her body went rigid.

No one had called her that in fourteen years. Not since the funeral that never was, not since the paperwork declared Vanessa Jordan dead in an accident that killed her mother and baby sister too.

His grip shifted, fingers digging into her jaw as he tilted her head back. The knife glinted. It wasn't at her throat yet, but tracing a slow line down the corner of her eye. Cold steel kissed skin, following the slope of her cheekbone.

When he leaned closer, she caught a whiff of a familiar scent. One that sucked her back in time.

Her father's office. Darkness. The muffled sound of a struggle. The coppery tang of blood in the air. She'd pressed her hands over her mouth, shaking so hard the hangers rattled in the closet. A man's voice, snarling something, and then the wet thud of steel meeting flesh. Again. Again.

The memory splintered as the masked man's blade reached her collarbone. "I saved you for last," he murmured, knuckles brushing the hollow of her throat. "A little reunion gift." His breath smelled of stale coffee.

Clara's face flashed in her mind. God, what would happen to her when Victoria was dead? Would this man find Clara and her mother too?

The knife pressed just below her jaw.

A gunshot cracked through the alley. The man jerked sideways with a sharp grunt, his grip faltering. Victoria didn't wait. She slammed her elbow into his ribs and twisted free, stumbling backward as he cursed, clutching his arm. Blood seeped between his fingers.

The masked man shoved her hard against the wall before bolting into the alley's shadows. Victoria gasped for air, bracing herself against the brick as her legs threatened to give out. She turned toward the street, where a woman with auburn hair, not unlike her own, stood with her gun still raised.

The woman didn't lower her weapon, her sharp eyes scanning the darkness where the attacker had fled. A black SUV roared up behind her, brakes screeching against damp pavement.

"Ms. Omstadt, my name is Jenna Briggs. I'm here to help you. Please, get in the car," the redhead said.

Victoria took a step back instead, pulse hammering. No way was she hopping into a stranger's vehicle, no matter who had just shot at her would-be killer. She'd seen enough thrillers to know how that ended.

The back door of the SUV swung open, and a man stepped out.

Victoria hesitated.

Her fingers clenched into fists. But then he moved into the dim streetlight, and something in the slope of his shoulders, the way he adjusted his glasses—god, those glasses—hitched in her memory like a snag in fabric.

He was taller now, broader in the shoulders, but his frame was still lean, his posture rigid like he wasn't sure how to stand in his own skin. He wore a dark suit, the jacket unbuttoned, tie slightly loosened. His light brown hair was shorter than she remembered, neatly styled but already mussed like he'd run his hands through it too many times.

And his hands—those same long, restless fingers that used to fidget with a Rubik's Cube in math class.

"Vanessa," he breathed.

Not Victoria.

Vanessa

She blinked, her breath shallow. "Penn?"

The streetlight caught the relief flickering across his face before he smoothed it out. He reached toward her but stopped halfway, hand hovering between them like he wasn't sure he was allowed. "It's me. And I swear to god, if you don't get in this car right now, I'm going to lose my mind."

Her chest tightened. She should run. She knew better than this.

But it was Penn.

Penn Levine. The quiet boy she'd befriended the year before her life went up in flames. The one she'd sat beside every lunch, nudging half her cafeteria food toward him because he never packed enough. The only person she'd regretted leaving when Vanessa Jordan died and Victoria Omstadt was born. Before the world burned.

"You were watching the show," she said, the realization dawning. A flicker of memory. He'd given her peonies before at the homecoming dance. He'd left unsigned notes in her locker. God, Penn was her phantom.

His throat worked. "Get in the car, Ness. Please."

The nickname unraveled something knotted in her ribs.

Jenna hadn't lowered her gun. "He might circle back."

Victoria stepped forward, and Penn's hand finally closed around hers, warm and familiar even after all this time. She grabbed her fallen bag, the spilled bouquet crushed underfoot, and let him guide her into the SUV. The second the door shut, Jenna slid into the passenger seat, and the vehicle lurched forward. A mountain of a man was in the driver's seat. He didn't say a word.

Victoria twisted, watching the alley shrink behind them, half-expecting the masked man to reappear.

Penn exhaled beside her, fingers tapping against his knee. "You okay?"

She turned to him, studying his face. The angles were sharper now, the faint stubble along his jaw, the bright eyes behind those glasses still too intense, too knowing.

"No," she admitted. "But I'm better than I was five minutes ago."

He swallowed before nodding. "Good. That's... good."

Jenna glanced back from the front seat. "Do you know who that man was, Ms. Omstadt?"

Victoria's stomach dropped. Right. The attack. The knife. The familiar scent that brought back too many memories. "If you're looking for a name. No. But I know who he is."

Jenna raised an eyebrow. "Who?"

"He's the man who killed my father and forced my mother, sister and me into witness protection."

———

VICTORIA WRAPPED HER HANDS AROUND THE STEAMING cup of chai tea. The scent—cardamom, cinnamon, just a touch of black pepper—made her breath catch.

He remembered.

Fifteen-year-old Vanessa had been picky about her tea. Steeped exactly four minutes, a splash of oat milk, honey instead of sugar. No one in her life now knew that. Not even Clara.

But Penn did.

She glanced up at him from beneath her eyelashes. He stood across the room, fingers twitching at his sides like he wanted to reach for something—a keyboard, a fidget spinner, anything to occupy his nervous energy. His lean frame was tense, shoulders stiff under the dress shirt, the sleeves rolled up to reveal his surprisingly strong forearms. His hazel eyes darted from her to the monitors lining the walls and back again.

"You've got no allergies listed in your current medical records," he said suddenly, nudging a pastry box toward her. "But I remembered— well, I think I remembered you were allergic to tree nuts. So the almond croissants are out. The blueberry muffins are safe."

"How do you know about my current medical records?" Victoria's fingers tightened around the mug.

Penn rubbed the back of his neck, staring up at the ceiling. His fingers flexed, then curled into loose fists. "I've, um, well, it's a long story."

"Penn."

"I've been watching you. For four years. I'm—I'm sorry, Ness."

The silence stretched.

Penn exhaled through his nose and tapped a key on his keyboard. A wall of screens flickered to life—photos, timestamps, security feeds. Victoria's stomach lurched. There she was, captured from every angle. Walking Sandy in Central Park. Leaving the theater late at night. Laughing with cast mates at a dimly lit pub.

Four years' worth of moments.

"What the hell?" Her skin prickled. "Penn, what the…Why?"

His jaw tightened. "Because I owed you."

"You stalked me because you owed me?"

Penn flinched. "Not—not like that. It was security monitoring. I set parameters. If you were in danger, I'd know." His voice dropped. "And tonight, you were."

The monitors changed again. Now, they showed grainy surveillance footage from the alley. The masked figure lunging, the glint of steel. Her own startled face, half-illuminated by the streetlight. Jenna's gunfire cracking through the dark.

Victoria's pulse hammered. "You watched that happen?"

Penn's fingers hovered over the keyboard. "Yeah."

Her stomach twisted. She should be furious. She *was* furious. But beneath the violation, something else nagged at her—an unsettling warmth at the realization that he'd been there, invisible, for every near-miss, every quiet moment.

"The flowers?"

"Your dad grew them in your backyard. You told me they were your favorite." Penn wouldn't meet her eye, putting his hands in his pockets and then taking them back out again.

"You've been to my shows."

"Every show."

Shit. What the hell was she supposed to do with this information? The man in front of her had taken it upon himself to watch her every move without her permission. To stalk her secretly. It was fucking creepy.

And yet.

He remembered her favorite flowers.

He remembered how she liked her tea.

He remembered her allergies.

And he'd just saved her damn life.

Penn leaned forward, gaze flicking to the ceiling before returning to her. "I know how this looks. But that man—I knew he was going to try again." He pulled up another image—enhanced, clearer. The stranger's profile, though the lower half of his face was still obscured. "He followed you the other night too. I saw his gun. I can't ID him yet because he's good at avoiding cameras, but he's been tailing you for weeks from what I can tell."

Victoria's throat went dry. "He called me Vanessa. Nobody... nobody has called me that in a long time. Until him."

"And me," Penn said, reading her reaction instantly. "God, Ness, shit, sorry. Victoria, I promise I'm not some creepy psychopath. I just...I wanted to have your back, like you had mine. Honestly, I was hoping you'd never find out."

Her grip on the mug turned white-knuckled. "But because of the man who killed my father, who is now coming after me, you were forced to tell the truth?"

Penn went completely still. "Yeah. I... yeah. I know I crossed too many boundaries, and I understand if you hate me now. And if you never want to see me again, I understand that too, but Ness. Shit, sorry. Victoria, you're in danger, and I just wanted to help and—"

"I don't hate you, Penn." She'd mumbled it, and he kept talking for a few seconds before it must've registered in that complex mind of his.

"You don't?" There was enough hope in those two words that her stomach twisted.

"I don't. I'm not saying what you did was right, but you weren't causing me or anyone else any harm. And it... it did save my life tonight." She took a deep breath, and when she met his expectant gaze, she offered him a small smile. "Thank you."

The relief that washed over Penn was almost tangible, the tension that had held him rigid seconds before uncoiling before her eyes. His shoulders dropped from where they'd been hunched near his ears. The constant, anxious motion of his hands stilled, and he let out a breath that sounded like it had been held for fourteen years. A faint, disbelieving smile touched his lips, vanishing as quickly as it appeared, replaced by a look of raw, unguarded awe.

She watched him, this man who was both a complete stranger and the painfully familiar boy from her past. The lean frame was taller, more defined, but he still had the same tendency to avoid direct eye contact, his gaze flicking from her face to the screens and back as if he couldn't process her presence without the mediation of his technology. The disheveled light brown hair was the same. He was still Penn, just... amplified.

"I thought..." He shook his head, a short, jerky movement. "After you were gone, I convinced myself I'd dreamed you up. That someone like you... couldn't have been real."

"Someone like me?" Victoria asked, taking a tentative sip of the tea. It was perfect.

"Someone who saw the kid everyone else kicked and decided he was worth saving." His fingers drifted toward a keyboard, but he pulled them back, shoving them into his pockets. "I remember the first time you saved me. They had me cornered near the bleachers. Three of them. I'd made the mistake of correcting the physics teacher in front of the whole class. They were going to make me eat my textbook. You stepped right between us," Penn continued, a note of wonder in his voice. "You told them to pick on someone their own size. You said I was the smartest person in that school, and they were just proving they were the dumbest." A faint, almost imperceptible chuckle escaped him. "You called the ringleader 'a fucking Nean-

24

derthal with a bad haircut.' He was so shocked, he just… walked away."

A smile touched Victoria's own lips. "He did have a terrible haircut."

"You checked on me every day after that. For months. You'd find me at lunch, ask if I'd eaten. You made me explain the computer science lessons to you in the library." He finally looked directly at her, his eyes intense behind his glasses. "And then one day, you just… weren't there. You were gone. Your locker was empty. No one knew anything. The teachers said you and your sister and mom had all died in a car accident."

The air left Victoria's lungs. She'd never known about that. WITSEC had manufactured a tragedy to sell the disappearance, to cauterize any loose ends.

"We… we went into protection," she said, tucking a strand of hair behind her ear. "The night my dad was… the night it happened. They came for us, bundled us into a car. We were given new names, new histories. We were told to never, ever look back. I'm sorry you thought that. I'm sorry you were alone."

Penn's Adam's apple bobbed as he swallowed. "It wasn't until years later. I was in college, messing around with dark web archives, old police blotters. I found the real report. Your father's assassination. Judge Gary Jordan. I put it together then." His voice softened. "I'm sorry about your dad."

"Thank you," she whispered. The old grief, a scar she thought had fully healed, throbbed anew. "If I could have… if there was any way I could have told you, said goodbye… I would have, Penn. You have to believe that. You weren't someone I just forgot."

He nodded, a quick, sharp dip of his chin, and looked away, blinking rapidly. Penn cleared his throat. His fingers twitched again, and he gestured vaguely at the bank of monitors, now showing a complex series of algorithms and data streams. "The man from the alley… he's not an amateur. The fact that he used your birth name means this is directly tied to your father's case. Your cover…" He hesitated, choosing his words carefully. "It's been compromised."

The warmth of the tea vanished, replaced by a deep, familiar chill. The fear she had spent over a decade running from was now sitting in the room with them, as real and tangible as the mug in her hands.

"I doubt that man will stop," Penn continued, his voice low, all trace of the nervous boy gone. "He'll try again." He finally turned to face her fully, his expression grave. "Let me help you. Let *us* help you. Crest Strategies... we can protect you. Well, Jenna and Jenna's people can protect you. And maybe I can find out who's behind this so you can put it all behind you. For good."

He took a step closer. "You don't have to run anymore, Ness. But you can't go back to your apartment. You can't go back to your life. Not yet. Will you let me help you?"

CHAPTER FOUR

PENN

PENN'S FINGERS DRUMMED AGAINST HIS THIGH. He watched the steam curl from Victoria's untouched tea—or was it Tori now? Ness? He still didn't know what to call her after all these years, and it felt like he kept screwing it up.

Her silence continued, and his pulse kicked up a notch. His ribs were steel bands around his lungs. She could refuse. She *should* refuse after what he'd admitted.

"Okay." One word, barely above a whisper.

His fingers stilled.

She looked up, emerald eyes bright with something that wasn't quite trust but wasn't fear either. "But I have conditions."

"Anything," he said, the word out before he could swallow it.

"My mother. And Clara." Victoria lifted her chin. "I want them protected too. However you protect me, I want you to—"

"Done. Yes. Of course." Penn didn't hesitate. He was already mapping the logistics, most of which were going to involve convincing Jenna to spare some more people. "You'll go to one of our safe houses."

A flicker of relief crossed her face. She straightened, a performer squaring her shoulders for the next act. "My dog has to go with me. I don't have anywhere else to take her and—"

"Okay."

"Oh. Good. And I need to go back to my apartment. I need clothes, cash, Sandy's—"

"No." The refusal jumped from him like a reflex. The alley replayed behind his eyes; the glint of the knife, how fast the attacker had moved. "It's not safe for you to go alone."

Victoria's eyes narrowed. "I'm not asking to go alone. I don't mind if you or that woman—"

"Jenna."

"Right, Jenna. I don't mind if someone goes with me, but I need to pick up some things first."

Penn flicked a glance at the closest monitor—the exterior of her building, live-feed green from night vision. Empty. For now. His fingers itched to pull up schematics. Instead, he tapped a key and spoke into a microphone on his desk. "Briggs. What's the status on the perimeter of Nes—Victoria's apartment?"

Jenna's voice crackled through. "My team says it's clear. No movement at the moment."

"Would it be safe for her and I to go and pick some things up before taking her to the safe house?"

Jenna's exhale was pure *you're an idiot*. "Fine. But I'm picking the team, and *I* drive. I'll meet you in ten minutes, rear garage." The line went dead.

Penn turned back to Victoria. His stomach twisted at the quiet gratitude in her expression. She was looking at him like he'd hung the moon again, and he'd burn down cities to keep that light in her eyes from guttering out.

————

PENN FOLLOWED VICTORIA INTO HER STUDIO APARTMENT, the threshold of her private world. It was a space he'd memorized in pixels, but never crossed in person except the one time he put in the hidden camera. The air smelled of jasmine and dog, cozy in a way no surveillance footage could ever capture. Sandy, the rescue mutt he'd watched trot loyally beside Victoria for years, stood in the entryway, ears pricked.

"She doesn't like most men," Victoria warned, stepping in first. "Don't make sudden moves or she might—"

Sandy bolted past her, tail whipping like a propeller. The dog shoved her snout into Penn's knee before he could react, sniffing hard, then let out a low, approving whine and licked his palm.

Victoria blinked. "That's... never happened before."

Penn crouched, gingerly offering his fingers. Sandy head-butted his chest hard enough to nearly knock him over. "Hi, gorgeous. Aren't you sweet?" He'd watched this dog nap on Victoria during thunderstorms, seen her grow from a skittish pup into the creature now pawing at him for belly rubs.

"Sandy, calm down."

Sandy did not calm down.

"I'm sorry. She's never reacted this way with a man before," Victoria said, placing her bag on the small counter.

"Guess she has good taste," he chuckled.

Victoria stared at the two of them as a smile tugged at her lips. "She never even liked my ex."

Penn's fingers stilled in Sandy's fur. The idea of Victoria dating left a bad feeling in his mouth. He cleared his throat. "You need to pack fast. Jenna's waiting. How can I help?"

Victoria moved toward her bed, Sandy trotting between them like a bridge. The apartment was smaller than he'd remembered. A well-worn reading chair shoved in the corner, a keyboard covered in sheet music, a bookshelf crammed with plays and dog-eared novels, and of course, the large bed taking up most of the room. He knew the layout, the routines—knew which floorboard creaked near the bathroom, the way the light hit the kitchen in the afternoon in every summer—but the *texture* of it all made his head spin. And the flowers. She had his bouquets everywhere.

Victoria yanked open a duffel bag and tossed him a smaller bag. "You can grab my toiletries. Bathroom's—"

"The only other door?" He asked, raising an eyebrow.

"Yeah, I know it's small, but—"

"I like it. It feels homey. Familiar." *Shit*. He hadn't meant to say that. "I'll just... I'll be in here."

He ducked into the bathroom. Four years of watching her pick mascara off this counter, of counting the breaths between her showers and rehearsals like they were lines of encryption. Now he was here, touching the toothpaste she used, the hairbrush with strands of auburn tangled in the bristles.

She called from the other room, "Can you make sure you grab my razor? It's in the shower."

Penn reached for Victoria's razor where it hung suction-cupped to the shower tile—and froze.

There, tucked discreetly behind her shampoo bottle, was a pink silicone vibrator.

His brain short-circuited. Heat roared up his neck. Four fucking years of surveillance, and he'd never—*Christ*. He hadn't let himself think about this. Hadn't *allowed* it. Watching was protection, not perversion. He'd skipped footage deliberately when she took care of herself. But he'd seen that very vibrator right before—

"Penn?" Victoria's voice came from the doorway, too close.

He snapped upright, wrist knocking the shampoo bottle. It clattered loudly against the tub. He fumbled to catch it, his pulse jackhammering.

"Got your razor." His voice sounded strangled.

She leaned against the doorframe, arms crossed. Sandy poked her head around Victoria's legs, panting up at him like she knew.

Victoria tilted her head. "Everything okay?"

Fine. Everything was fine except the blood currently making executive decisions far south of his brain. He shoved the razor into her toiletry bag, willing his heartbeat to steady.

"Yeah. Just—dropped something." He didn't meet her eyes, adjusting his stance subtly to alleviate the pressure in his pants.

Fuck, the only thing he could think of was the variety of ways he could use that vibrator to make Victoria come over and over again. And that was not helping with the straining dick he was trying to hide.

Victoria hummed, stepping forward to grab toothpaste off the sink —brushing past him. Jasmine scent, warmth radiating off her skin.

Penn exhaled sharply through his nose and stared at the ceiling like it held the secrets of the universe. *Think about firewalls. Think about Tanner's disappointed face.*

"Oh, that's where that is. Can't forget that." Victoria scooped the vibrator into her bag without hesitation, no flicker of embarrassment.

"We should hurry," he muttered, fleeing the bathroom before his body betrayed him further. "Jenna's waiting in the car."

When he returned to the main room, Sandy immediately glued herself to his leg. Victoria followed him out and shoved a stack of folded clothes into the bag. "She's adopting you. Hope you're a dog person."

He wasn't. He'd never had pets. But Sandy leaned her full weight against him, trusting and warm, and something in him cracked open.

"Need anything else?" His voice came out hoarse.

Victoria glanced around. "My laptop. Chargers." She hesitated, then strode to a framed photo on the bookshelf—a teenage girl with curls and a gap-toothed grin, clinging to Victoria's back in what had to be a decade-old snapshot. Clara. Penn had never seen it this close.

Victoria tucked it carefully into the bag with the last remaining items. "Okay. Let's go."

Jenna was already tapping her fingers on the SUV's steering wheel when they emerged. Penn got in first, and Sandy hopped in after, turning around twice before sitting directly on Penn's lap. Thank god his erection was gone. Victoria hugged the duffel to her chest. She stayed quiet as the city blurred past. Penn clenched his jaw, fighting the urge to pull up every camera in a five-mile radius on his phone, to scour every shadow for movement.

The safe house was a nondescript brownstone with a biometric lock. Jenna lingered at the door, arms crossed. "There is food in the fridge. Emergency protocols on the tablet. Call if you see anything weirder than Penn's face."

Victoria huffed a laugh. Penn flushed.

"Dani and Lucas are going to stay outside tonight, and my people will rotate through. Most of the time, you won't know they're here. But they will be, and they won't step in unless they have to." Jenna put her hands on her hips. "We've got the same deal going on for your sister and mother. Your sister will be escorted to and from school, just like you'll have an escort any time you want to leave."

"So, house arrest?" Victoria ran her hands over her arms.

Jenna chuckled. "Something like that. Penn, do you want me to wait?"

Penn glanced at Victoria, and then down at Sandy. "Yeah. I'll just make sure she gets settled and then I'll leave with you."

"Sounds good. Ms. Omstadt, you have my number in case anything happens. "Let him know if you need anything else." Jenna pointed her thumb sideways towards Penn. "Consider him your personal genie in a bottle."

"Briggs," Penn said, clearing his throat. He didn't need the image of Victoria rubbing him like a genie's lamp. Not after that fucking vibrator.

"Okay, I'll wait by the car. Goodnight, Ms. Omstadt." Jenna gave a two-finger salute and trotted down the stairs to where the SUV sat.

"Can I help with the bag?" Penn asked, and Victoria thanked him, handing him the overstuffed duffel.

The safe house smelled like lemon polish and fresh linen. Penn toed off his shoes at the door, feet sinking into the plush carpet as he carried Victoria's duffel down the hallway. He knew this place; had designed its security system himself. But seeing Victoria in it made the space feel alien.

"Where do you want this?" he asked, hovering near the master bedroom door.

"I don't know. There is fine." Victoria seemed too busy looking around the place. "God, this house is huge. Definitely looks bigger from the inside."

Sandy circled the living room once before flopping onto the rug with an exaggerated sigh. Jenna leaned against the doorframe to the master bedroom, arms crossed.

"I think you could fit at least three of my apartments in here. What am I supposed to do with all this space?"

"Throw a party?" Penn cleared his throat. "That's a joke. Don't actually throw a party. It wouldn't be safe because—"

"I know it was a joke, Penn."

"Right, um, well, the security protocols are on the tablet by the bed. Fingerprint locks on every window. There's a panic button under—"

"The kitchen counter. I know how safe houses work."

Right. Because of course she did. WITSEC kid. Fuck.

He rubbed the back of his neck. "Right. So. I'll be monitoring from the command center. Call if you—"

Victoria stepped forward and hugged him.

It happened so fast he barely had time to process. The warmth of her body against his, the press of her cheek against his shoulder, the faint scent of hairspray still clinging to her hair. His arms hung frozen at his sides for a second before instinct took over and he hugged her back.

"For the record," she murmured against his shirt, "I looked you up, too."

His breath caught.

"You had a LinkedIn. And a—a Twitter account with three tweets from 2012." She pulled back just enough to meet his eyes, her fingers gripping the fabric of his sleeves. "I just wanted to make sure you were okay. That you were—" Alive. Happy. Neither of them said it. "I couldn't contact you. Not with WITSEC. But I checked. A lot. At least at first."

Penn's throat tightened. All this time, he thought he was the only one watching.

She squeezed his arms gently. "And thank you. For the flowers."

He blinked. "You deserve them."

Her cheeks flushed.

Penn shoved his hands in his pockets as he backed towards the door, managing to avoid the dog, who didn't give a single fuck about moving even when Penn had to step over her. "Right. Well, I... Um... I should go." He paused at the doorway. "You know, Jenna is waiting, and you're probably exhausted, and—"

"Goodnight, Penn." Victoria reached up on her tiptoes and kissed him on the cheek. "Thank you."

His pulse kicked against his ribs. He managed a stiff nod before bolting out the door. The chilly night air hit him, and he waited for her to close the front door. As soon as she did, Penn stalled on the brownstone steps, running both hands through his hair as if he could physically rearrange the chaos in his head.

Jenna slapped his shoulder as he passed by her. "Smooth exit, Romeo."

"Shut up."

"You're so fucked."

"Yeah," he muttered. "I know."

CHAPTER FIVE

VICTORIA

VICTORIA TOSSED ONTO HER OTHER SIDE FOR WHAT FELT like the hundredth time. The bed was enormous—too big, too empty. Sandy let out a disgruntled *whuff* from the foot of the bed, annoyed at the constant movement, before jumping down with a thump and a pointed sigh.

She stared at the vaulted ceiling, fingers sliding against the unfamiliar sheets. Safe house or not, the silence was too heavy. Too full of everything she didn't want to think about—her father's laugh, the way his voice cracked when he sang off-key in the car. The terror in his voice when he'd hidden her in the closet. The sound of his pleading and his cries of pain. The silence afterward.

And then there was *him*.

Penn Levine.

Scrawny, awkward little Penn with his too-big glasses and a bruise on his cheekbone from where some asshole upperclassman had shoved him into a locker. She'd heard him in the boys' bathroom crying after school one day, barely fourteen, shaking so bad he couldn't even grip the sink. Back then, she'd been Vanessa, too bold for her own damn good, marching right into the boys' restroom like she owned it.

She had checked on him every single day. Made sure he had someone to sit with in the cafeteria and in class. Made sure he knew someone saw him.

Now, fourteen years later, he'd watched her every performance.

Made sure she knew someone saw her.

Victoria pressed the heels of her hands into her eyes, exhaling hard.

That wasn't the same boy in the bathroom. Or the empty kid on the roof of the high school. The man tonight had shoulders that filled out his shirt like he spent hours doing something other than coding (and god, she had felt them when she hugged him). His jaw was sharper, his posture taller. No trace of the hunch that used to make him look half his height. But those eyes. They were the same. And that small grin he gave her right before he pushed his glasses up the bridge of his nose.

Her skin prickled.

Fuck, she needed to sleep.

She shouldn't be thinking about this. Not now. Not after the attack tonight. But her body wasn't listening. God forbid it actually follow her commands.

Victoria turned over again, the sheets tangling around her legs. The mattress was too soft, the room too quiet. Every time she closed her eyes, she saw Penn. Not the boy from high school, not the ghost she'd carried in her memory, but the man he'd become. His hands. God, his hands. They'd looked so different now. Larger, stronger, fingers deft as they worked the keyboard in the car or adjusted his glasses. What could those hands do to her? Those long fingers. The thought sent a shiver down her spine, heat pooling low in her belly.

Her cheeks burned, and she buried her face in the pillow. This was ridiculous. She'd just been attacked, for Christ's sake. Her life was in danger, her family's safety was at risk, and here she was, lying in bed, her body betraying her with thoughts of Penn's fingers working her into a frenzy. She squeezed her eyes shut, but the image of Penn lingered. His hazel eyes behind those glasses, the way his voice had softened when he called her "Ness" again. And earlier, in her apartment, she'd seen him notice her vibrator. Saw the way he froze for half a second before averting his gaze, his ears turning pink under his messy hair.

She groaned, shoving the pillow over her face. "Stop it," she muttered, but her body wasn't listening. Her skin felt too tight, too sensitive, and she couldn't stop wondering what he'd thought when he saw it. If he'd imagined her using it. If he'd imagined himself using it on her.

"Fuck," she hissed, kicking the sheets off. She was wound so tight she could barely breathe, and she was not dealing with this right now. But the more she tried to ignore it, the worse it got. Her thighs pressed together, and she swore under her breath again. Fine. Fine. If this was the only way she was going to get any sleep, then so be it.

She sat up, running a hand through her hair. Sandy lifted her head from the floor, tilting it at her with a questioning look. "Out," she said, pointing to the door. Sandy didn't move. "Sandy, out. Mom needs some alone time."

The dog huffed, as if she knew exactly what Victoria was about to do, but she obeyed, trotting out of the bedroom with what Victoria swore was judgment in her posture. Victoria swung her legs over the side of the bed, locking the door. She wasn't about to risk her dog walking in on her like some kind of deranged pervert.

Crossing the room to where she'd unpacked her bag, Victoria rummaged through it until she found what she was looking for. The vibrator was sleek pink silicone, and was embarrassingly familiar in her hand. She hesitated for a moment, glancing at herself in the mirror across the room. Her hair was a mess, her eyes wide and a little wild, but she couldn't stop thinking about Penn's face when he'd seen it. The way his Adam's apple had bobbed when he swallowed. The way his pupils had dilated. Darkened.

She climbed back into bed, the cool sheets against her skin making her shiver. She lay back, staring at the ceiling, but her mind was already racing. His hands. His eyes. The way he'd called her Ness. The way he'd watched her for years, knowing every detail of her life, her routines, her favorites. It should have been creepy. It should have made her skin crawl. It should have been the last thing to make her skin tight and her thighs clench.

But all she could think about was how much he'd cared. How much he'd risked to keep her safe.

She turned the vibrator on, the low hum filling the room. Her breath hitched as she pressed it against her thigh, the vibrations making her skin tingle. She closed her eyes, and Penn's face was there, clear as day. His sharp jaw, his messy hair, the way his lips parted slightly when he was deep in thought. She imagined his hands on her, rough and gentle all at once, tracing the curve of her hip, the dip of her waist, the swell of her breast. Her free hand mimicked his hand in her mind, following the trail imaginary Penn left. She remembered his low voice whispering her name.

Her real name.

Her fingers moved of their own accord, trailing up her stomach to her breasts, and she bit her lip to stifle a moan. She imagined Penn's mouth there instead, his teeth grazing her skin, his hands sliding down her body. She pressed the vibrator against her clit, her back arching off the bed as the pleasure shot through her. It wasn't enough. It wasn't him.

She adjusted the setting, the vibrations intensifying, and her breath came in short, sharp gasps. She thought of his face when he'd hugged her earlier, the way his body had felt against hers—solid, safe, warm. She thought of the way he'd looked at her in the car, like she was the only person in the world. Like she was the only thing that mattered.

Her hips moved against the vibrator, the pleasure building, coiling tighter and tighter. She imagined his hands sliding between her legs, his fingers replacing the toy, his mouth against her neck as he whispered her name. She imagined him watching her, his eyes dark with desire, his breath ragged as she fell apart beneath him.

"Penn," she gasped, her voice breaking on the word. Her body tensed, pleasure crashing over her in waves, and she bit down on her hand to keep from crying out. His face was all she could see, his name the only thing on her lips as she came, her body shuddering.

When the tremors subsided, she lay there, breathing hard, the vibrator still buzzing softly in her hand. She turned it off, the sudden silence almost deafening. Her heart was pounding in her chest, her skin flushed and sensitive. She stared at the ceiling, her mind spinning.

What the hell had just happened?

She shoved the vibrator under the pillow, pulling the sheets up to her chin. She felt… strange. Exposed. Vulnerable. And not just because of what she'd just done. Because it wasn't just some random fantasy. It wasn't some anonymous figure in her head. It was Penn.

Rolling onto her side, she tucked her knees up to her chest. Her breathing slowly evened out, the tension in her body easing. The room was quiet, the only sound the soft ticking of the clock on the wall. Her eyelids grew heavy, and she started to drift, her thoughts becoming hazy. But even as sleep claimed her, his face lingered in her mind. His name on her lips.

Penn.

———

THE SCENT OF PEONIES HIT VICTORIA THE MOMENT SHE opened the door, nudging Sandy out of the way. Penn stood there, his arms full of white blooms, slightly crushed against his chest as if he'd been clutching them too tightly on the way over. His hair was still damp. Either from a shower or the early morning rain. He had faint shadows of sleeplessness under his eyes, but he was otherwise put together. Crisp dark sweater. jeans, that sharp jawline that had occupied her dreams far too vividly last night.

Her stomach did a slow, treacherous swoop.

"Morning." He said, clearing his throat like he hadn't spoken to anyone yet today. He shifted his grip on the flowers. "Thought, uh. You might want them in person this time."

Her palms tingled. She curled them into her robe to hide the reaction. "You thought right."

She stepped aside to let him in, her skin prickling as he brushed past her. The faint scent of his shower gel—something woodsy, clean —mixed with the flowers, and her heart hammered. She could still see him in her mind, the way she'd pictured him last night, breath hot on her skin, fingers knuckle deep inside her as she cried out his name.

Stop it. She exhaled sharply through her nose and took the bouquet from him before she could do something stupid, like bury her face in them. "Thank you."

"You sleep okay?"

Her fingers spasmed around the stems.

That flush she'd been battling shot straight up her neck, her cheeks igniting. She turned sharply toward the kitchen without answering, shoving the flowers into the first empty container she found—a pitcher, too short, the blooms lolling awkwardly over the rim. Shit. She should trim them, put them in water, something. But her mind was a mess.

She risked a glance over her shoulder.

Penn was standing exactly where she'd left him in the entryway, hands tucked into his pockets, gaze fixed on her with quiet intensity.

Oh God. He knows.

"You want coffee?" Victoria blurted out, desperate to claw back some semblance of control.

His brow twitched, but he didn't push. "Yeah. Thanks."

"Come in," she said, watching as Sandy trotted up to him and shoved her nose in his crotch. "Sandy, knock it off."

Penn chuckled, patting her dog on the head as he shut the door. "You didn't answer my question. How'd you sleep?"

She busied herself with the coffee machine, gripping the counter like it might ground her. And thank god for acting, because she managed to sound normal—or close enough—when she finally answered his question. "Slept fine. Weird dreams, but that's not new."

That much at least was true.

She could feel him watching her.

"You still drink it black?" She pushed a mug toward him without waiting for an answer, then leaned back against the counter with her own, blowing lightly across the top.

"Yeah. Good memory." Penn sipped his coffee. He didn't seem in any hurry to speak, and that, more than anything, unnerved her.

Her fingers gripped the mug. "So. What's the plan?"

"Your call." He set his coffee down. "Figured we should talk about work first."

"My work?"

"Your show." He tilted his head. "I'm guessing you want to go back?"

A tiny knot loosened in her chest. "If I can," she said carefully. "I mean—I don't know how safe it is. You'd know better than me."

His gaze flickered. "We can make sure you get there and back safely. So you don't want to stop?"

She ran her thumb along the rim of her cup. "I love performing. It's not just a job, it's—" She swallowed. "It's the only time I get to stop being me for a while."

Penn went still.

Victoria traced a fingertip through the condensation on her mug, not looking at him. "When I'm on stage, I don't have to think about anything else. I don't have to be Victoria Omstadt. Or Vanessa Jordan." She flicked the droplet off her skin. "I can be someone else."

Something shifted in Penn's expression, and he gave an understanding nod. "I get it. That's why I played video games in high school. I got to be the hero, or the villain. Anyone but me. I'll talk to Briggs. We'll figure security out."

She exhaled in relief. "Thank you. I appreciate your caring enough to even consider it."

"You're talented," he said with a shrug and a sheepish smile "I selfishly want to keep watching you perform." His words made the infuriating blush return to her cheeks. He straightened, pulling at his collar. "But rehearsal today's optional, and there's no show tonight."

She blinked. "You know my schedule."

"Surveillance." His lips twitched. "Told you. Four years."

God, that should've been creepy. Unfortunately, her twisted mind just recognized that he cared enough to check. Fuck, she was messed up.

"So if you're free," he said, biting his lower lip, "I was thinking you might want to come to my lab." He rubbed the back of his neck, fingers flexing like he wasn't sure what to do with his hands. "We can go through what I've got on the guy who came after you. There's a chance you might recognize something."

Her pulse jumped. His lab. His domain. A little piece of him for her to explore.

"...Okay."

He didn't smile, exactly, but something in his posture softened. "Good."

She set her mug down, half-finished. "Give me twenty minutes. I just need to take a quick shower and get dressed."

Penn nodded, stepping back toward the door. "I'll wait in the car."

No. No no no—

She bit her lip. "You could stay. If you want." The words were out before she could stop them.

He paused, giving her a once-over. Ah, shit. Why hadn't she bothered to put on real clothes? A robe wasn't clothes.

Her pulse hammered. "I mean—if you're just going to be sitting in the car anyway—"

Penn exhaled. His fingers tapped once against the doorframe.

"Okay. I'll just... I'll sit with Sandy."

"Great. Cool." Victoria swallowed. Deep breaths. Just breathe through it. She turned and walked—calmly, normally, oh god—toward the bedroom.

She didn't look back.

She didn't need to.

She could feel him watching.

CHAPTER SIX

PENN

PENN'S FINGERS DRUMMED AGAINST THE STEERING WHEEL. He could feel Victoria beside him in the passenger seat—*too close, too close*—even though she wasn't touching him. He hadn't been this aware of another person's presence since... well. *Ever*.

Shit. This was a mistake.

He cast a sharp glance at her profile. Victoria's gaze stayed fixed on the passing city. What the hell was she thinking? He could hack into any database, crack any firewall, but this—her head tipping upwards as she studied the street signs, the way her fingers played at the edge of her jacket—this was an entirely unsolvable code.

And now he was taking her to the place no one but Carson and the other Crest Strategies had ever stepped foot in. His sanctuary. His obsession, laid bare in monitors and wiring.

Fuck.

When they arrived and the warehouse door slid shut behind them with a quiet *hiss*, sealing them in the neon glow of his screens, Penn held his breath, waiting for her reaction.

"Holy shit," Victoria whispered.

His throat went dry.

She stepped forward as if she were walking into some sacred place. "Penn... this is all yours?"

His fingers clenched at his sides, and he flicked his gaze to the drawer where he'd put his fidget spinner. He needed it. Or something. Anything to distract his anxious thoughts. "Yeah."

She turned in a slow circle, taking in the chaos. He'd spent three hours cleaning the space before he'd gone to her that morning. Still, what if it wasn't enough? What if he'd missed a wrapper or an empty energy drink can? Penn scanned the area as a precaution, but the control room was cleaner than it had been in months. The monitors flickered with code; the custom rigs hung this way and that.

Her fingers brushed the back of his chair, and his brain short-circuited. Fuck, she was really in his lab.

"You did all this?"

His pulse roared in his ears. "Uh. Yeah."

A soft, disbelieving laugh escaped her. "You've done really well for yourself. This must've cost multiple fortunes."

He swallowed hard. She had no idea. He didn't tell her that the same brain that made him a target in school was the one that had made him billions of dollars over the years. That his net worth had enough zeros to buy this fucking warehouse a hundred times over.

None of that mattered.

Not when she was looking at him like that—like he had actually done something worth admiration.

She wandered deeper into the space, her fingers trailing along the edges of his equipment. He tracked her every movement, his mind betraying him with every fantasy he'd imagined in the last four years.

He could bend her over that workstation. Or that one. Could press her against the glass wall where the city lights echoed behind her and drive her fucking wild with that damn vibrator while he fucked her in the ass. Could take her apart on the fucking floor right now, until her breathing matched the frantic rhythm of his code. Could show her the cabinet where he kept his own toys. The ropes. The whips. The chains.

If she didn't run now, she'd certainly run then.

His skin burned.

Fuck. *Fuck.* He needed to focus.

He turned sharply toward the nearest terminal, pulling up the case files before his body could do something mortifying. The screen flickered to life. Photographs, reports, security stills—all organized in a way that likely only made sense to him. He forced air into his lungs.

Victoria was behind him in seconds. "Is this—?"

"Yeah." His voice came out rougher than he meant it to, and he cleared his throat. "Old case files. Police reports. Everything I could dig up about your father."

She leaned in, so close her hair brushed his shoulder. He caught the damn scent of her shampoo, and he had to white-knuckle the edge of the desk just to keep from turning into her. To keep from dragging her closer and drinking her in until he was drunk on her.

Her brow furrowed as she skimmed the records. "Detective Albert Morrison?"

"He was the primary investigator." He tapped a key, and the file expanded. They were morning reports, interview transcripts, a grainy photo of a tired-looking detective with a five-o'clock shadow. "Closed the case as 'ongoing' for, uh. A while."

"I remember him." Victoria exhaled, biting her bottom lip. Damn it. He wanted to bite her bottom lip. "He never solved it."

"Yeah. There are a lot of cases that go unsolved, unfortunately."

Her fingers curled into fists. Penn hesitated, then—stupidly, recklessly—he let his own fingers brush against the back of her hand. Just once. She didn't pull away. Didn't flinch.

"How did you even get all of this?"

"Some of it I'd already looked into four years ago. And the rest of it..." He shrugged. "Well, I didn't sleep last night." Penn didn't add that he didn't sleep because every time he closed his eyes, she was there, under him. Around him. Moaning his name.

Victoria turned to face him. "Why?"

He offered her a small smile and pushed his glasses up his nose. "I had work to do."

Her gaze trailed over his expression, resting longer on his lips for a beat longer before traveling back up to his eyes. She returned his smile. "Show me the rest."

They worked like that for hours. Shoulder to shoulder, dissecting every lead, every dead end. He could sense every breath she took, every shift of her body against his. There was a good chance he would perish from restraint before they were through.

When she started yawning, he ordered food without asking.

Her eyes widened when she saw the bag. "Is that—?"

"Chicken tikka masala." He shoved it toward her. "Extra cilantro. And—uh." He pulled out the small, carefully packaged box. "Kulfi."

Victoria went very, very still. "God, you remember everything, don't you?"

"Everything about you, yeah." He leaned against one of the work-tables, his hands in his pockets as he dropped her gaze. "You... You were my only friend, Ness. I didn't have to remember anything about anyone else because there was no one else."

"Penn..." She frowned, opened her mouth, and then closed it. "I—"

"Anyway, there's also naan bread in there too. I'll grab drinks." He scratched the back of his head, walking towards the fridge. It wasn't that he didn't want to hear what she had to say next. There was a very good chance he could survive and even thrive on just her words and her voice alone. Okay, well, maybe not physically, but still. He just didn't want to hear the pity in her voice. He knew he had had a rough time growing up. He didn't need to be reminded. Didn't need someone to try to paint it differently. She'd been his only friend, the only light in his darkness, and he was fine remembering it that way.

So yes. Of course he fucking remembered. He remembered every-thing—how she used to peel the stickers off her schoolbooks in perfect squares, how she always tied her shoelaces in double knots, how she'd hum show tunes under her breath when she didn't think anyone was listening. He remembered the way she'd handed him that mango kulfi on a sweltering summer day, back when he was still just some lame broken kid.

"Try it," she'd said. "You'll like it."

He'd liked anything she gave him.

Penn returned with two bottles of sparkling water. Grapefruit for her, lime for him.

Victoria peeled open the dessert, her smile just the way he remembered. "Thank you. For the food, I mean. And for helping with all of this." She gestured to the wall of monitors.

Penn just nodded, throat too tight to speak. He watched Victoria take the first bite of kulfi, the way her lips closed around the spoon, the faint hum of pleasure that escaped her. He'd replayed that sound in his head a thousand times; her voice, her laughter, the soft hitch of her breath when something surprised her. But hearing it now, in real time, in *his* space. It was fucking lethal.

He forced himself to look away, tearing off a piece of naan with more force than necessary.

"You never told me," she said after a moment, swirling her spoon in the dessert, "how you ended up at Crest."

Penn shrugged, keeping his eyes on his food. "Carson found me."

"That's it?"

"He needed someone who could break into systems without leaving a trace. I was... good at that." He glanced up, catching the way her brow furrowed. "What?"

"You make it sound like he just plucked you off the street."

"Not far off." He smirked, but it didn't reach his eyes. "I was in a bad place. I... um... I had been arrested for hacking into something I should not have, and when he heard about it, he tracked me down and bailed me out."

"Arrested, huh?"

Penn tore another piece of naan, crumbs scattering across the desk. "FBI servers. I got sloppy. Left a backdoor that flagged their alarms."

Victoria's spoon stopped halfway to her mouth, eyes widening. "You hacked the FBI?"

"The Pentagon was harder." The corner of his mouth twitched. "I'm kidding. I just wanted to peek at the FBI's payroll system. Wanted to see if my last foster parents were still collecting checks for me." A bitter laugh escaped him. "Turns out, they were."

Silence settled between them, as Penn remembered yet another low point in his life. He could still taste the stale coffee from that interrogation room, the way his hands shook as he waited for sentencing. Then Carson Crest walked in wearing a one of a kind charcoal suit and a cunning smile.

"Carson showed up like some fucking corporate vigilante," Penn continued. "Bailed me out, then offered me a job five minutes later." His fingers traced the condensation on his water bottle. "'I can make all this disappear,' he told me. 'Or I can make *you* disappear into a federal prison.'" Penn imitated Carson's cocky voice, smirking at the water bottle. "Arrogant asshole."

"Jesus, Penn."

"I thought it was a con at first. But Cars..." His throat tightened. "It wasn't just the money or the tech. For the first time, someone valued what I could do. No one was gonna kick me out if my code had bugs or if I stayed up too late rewriting protocols. The others—Benedict, Tanner, James—they didn't give a shit that I couldn't do small talk or that I flinched when someone touched me."

His pulse hammered as he met her gaze. "They kept me. Even when I was a nightmare. Even when I fucked up."

Victoria reached across the space between them, her fingertips brushing his wrist. It lit every nerve in his body. "I'm glad you found them," she whispered.

"Yeah, me too."

She pulled back, but her gaze remained on him. "You were always brilliant, Penn. Even back in high school."

His chest tightened. She had no idea what those words did to him. How they unraveled something deep and desperate inside him. He wanted to crawl into the praise and live there.

"Yeah, well." He cleared his throat. "Brilliant doesn't pay the bills unless someone's willing to exploit it."

Her gaze flickered over his face, searching. "You said you thought about me a couple times, right? After I—"

"Every day." The words were out before he could stop them. Fuck. Too much. Too honest. He busied himself with his food, but he could feel her staring at him. But it was out there now, and it was too late. He swallowed hard, and then continued. "I would've followed you, Ness. Anywhere."

Her lips parted.

Goddamnit, those fucking lips. He wanted to taste those lips more than he wanted anything. Penn's breath hitched as Victoria leaned in, her knee brushing against his beneath the desk. His skin prickled. Every shift of her body, every fleeting glance at his mouth sent a spike of awareness through him.

Her fingers lingered near his wrist, a ghost of a touch that left him aching. He should look away. Should force himself to focus on the case files still glowing on the screens around them. But he couldn't.

Victoria was staring at him.

Like somehow against all reason she felt this too.

Her long lashes dipped, gaze flicking to his mouth before darting back to his eyes. His pulse thundered. His throat tightened. He was hyperaware of everything—the warmth of her breath, the scent of her shampoo, the way her tongue darted out to wet her bottom lip like she was imagining—

Don't. Don't do this to yourself.

His hands trembled in his lap, fingers flexing, itching to reach for her. To drag her closer. But his brain was already spiraling. Too many thoughts, too many variables. *She's compromised. She's scared. She's reacting to adrenaline, to gratitude, not to you, not like—*

She tilted her head, just slightly.

Breath catching, he mirrored her without thinking. Closer. *Closer.*

Her lips parted.

His brain short-circuited. He'd fantasized about this in a thousand ways ever since high school. Ever since he'd met the one person who'd seen him when he'd tried to make himself invisible. He'd imagined how she might taste, how her fingers might tighten in his shirt, how she might sigh into his mouth. And now that it might be real... his body locked up, torn between desperation and sheer, overwhelming panic.

Not like this. Not when she's vulnerable. Not when you—

One of his monitors beeped.

Reality snapped back into focus like he'd just put on his glasses.

Penn jolted, tearing his gaze away just as Victoria flinched, blinking like she too had forgotten where they were. The monitor flashed red, signaling another failed match in his facial recognition scan.

"Shit," he muttered automatically, dragging a hand through his hair. He got up and moved to the keyboard connected to the monitor, typing up the commands to begin the next search with new parameters.

Penn clenched his fists after starting the next search. That *beep* had saved him from doing something monumentally stupid.

And yet—

He wanted to throw the damn computer out the window.

CHAPTER SEVEN

VICTORIA

Victoria traced the edge of her teacup, watching the steam curl into the air. Twenty-five days. It felt like a lifetime spent in this beautifully appointed cage. The brownstone's security system hummed to remind her that the world outside held teeth.

Penn had come by again early that morning. White peonies, as always. He'd wanted to check on her before he went in to the office and had only stayed fifteen minutes, running a diagnostic on the security panel by the door, his fingers flying over the keypad while he congratulated her on her performance the night before. Of course he'd gone. She'd looked for him during the last few performances, but with the stage lights, it was nearly impossible to make out faces. Penn left after making a final sweep of the safe house, promising to be back with lunch later.

A soft chime from her phone pulled her out of her thoughts. It was a notification from the theater. Costume adjustments tomorrow, 2 PM. She typed a quick reply, then opened a second app Penn had installed for her to reach Jenna and her team. A single tap sent an automated alert to Crest Strategies, notifying them of her scheduled movement. Seamless. Invisible. One of Jenna's people, another woman, had been introduced to the cast as Victoria's cousin from out of town, dropping her off every day. Another woman had joined the crew to watch Victoria backstage during the performances. A third would meet her at the stage door when she finished. No one questioned any of it.

The performance was her anchor, the one piece of her old life they let her keep. The familiar weight of Meg's various wigs, the smell of stage dust and fog juice, the collective breath of the audience—it was the only time the constant, pricking sense of watchfulness faded. She could lose herself in the choreography, in the music. She could almost forget the man with the knife who knew her birth name.

Her phone buzzed again, skittering on the marble countertop. An unknown number. Her heart gave a hard, painful thump against her ribs. She stared at the screen, her breath caught in her throat.

It buzzed again. Then, a third time.

She picked it up slowly. "Hello?"

"It's Dani." The voice was calm. One of Jenna's team. "Just did the outer perimeter sweep. All clear. You good?"

Victoria exhaled, the tension bleeding from her shoulders. "Yeah. I'm good. Thanks, Dani."

The line went dead. Victoria set the phone down, her hand trembling slightly. This was her life now. A life of coded check-ins and armed women pretending to be her friends. A life where a wrong number could freeze the blood in her veins.

She looked at the peonies standing tall and perfect in a crystal vase. Penn's silent, daily apology. His promise. She ran a finger over a velvety petal.

He was trying so hard to fix this. To keep her safe. But as the days bled into one another in this gilded prison, a restless energy was building inside her. She was tired of being the one who was watched.

Victoria drained the last of her tea, licking the faint honey from her lips before setting the cup down. Sandy bounded across the living room, tail wagging furiously, and dropped her favorite chew toy—a battered giraffe now missing an ear—into Victoria's lap.

She grinned, scratching behind the dog's ears. "Yeah, okay, you monster."

Victoria stretched out on the plush rug, lying back as Sandy half-climbed onto her stomach, gnawing the toy with exaggerated growls. The late-morning sunlight streamed through the blinds, painting stripes across the hardwood floor. For a second, it almost felt normal.

Her phone sat within reach, and she hesitated only a moment before swiping it open. She tapped the contact named *Little Miss Nerd (Do Not Ignore)*, twisting a strand of her hair around one finger as the call connected.

Clara answered on the second ring, her voice bright. "You never call this early unless something's wrong."

Victoria exhaled a laugh. "Maybe I just missed you."

"Yeah, right." A keyboard clattered in the background. "Also, I know that sigh. What happened?"

Victoria rolled onto her side, flicking Sandy's ear. "Nothing *happened*. Just checking in."

The typing paused. "Uh-huh." A beat. "You're still in the safe house?"

"Mm. You?"

"Yeah. It's fancy, V. You sure this isn't, like, some weird billionaire cult? You didn't sell yourself as a sex slave to get us new digs, did you? Oh, god, you did, didn't you? Does your safe house have a sex dungeon?"

Victoria choked on nothing. "Jesus, Clara."

"Look, all I'm saying is, if they offer you a magic serum, run. Well, unless the billionaire you made a deal with has a large dick. Then I guess you could stay. Does he have a—"

"Clara." The corner of Victoria's mouth twitched. "Not a cult. Not a sex slave. And I'm not getting any giant billionaire dick. I shouldn't even be talking to you about this. You're just a teenager." Victoria wrinkled her nose.

"I'm old enough to know that you're drier than the desert."

"I'm going to pretend you didn't say that."

Clara chuckled, but when she spoke again, her voice was quieter "Did Mom call you yet?"

Victoria stilled. Sandy nosed at her hand, but she barely felt it. "No."

"She asked about you yesterday."

"Yeah?"

"Yeah." Clara sighed. "She was having a good day. Made pasta from scratch and everything. Then she just—stopped. All of the sudden, she just kinda... shut down."

Victoria closed her eyes, pressing her forehead to Sandy's warm fur. Their mother hadn't fully come back after the murder. Some days, she was almost like she used to be—laughing, humming old songs, teasing Clara about her latest gaming obsession. Other days, she was a ghost, moving through life without seeing it.

"I'll call her," Victoria murmured.

"Good luck getting her to pick up."

The bitterness in Clara's voice was new. Victoria frowned. "Hey."

"What?"

"You okay?"

"I just wish you were here. She makes it difficult to be around her most of the time. I think the switch to this safe house just triggered something in her. I just... I miss you."

A lump formed in Victoria's throat. "I miss you too."

When Clara spoke again, she'd clearly injected more lightness into her voice. It was fake, and Victoria recognized it, but she didn't push. "Are you ever planning on visiting me ever? This safe house has a pool. Or is your hot billionaire not letting you leave?"

Victoria rolled her eyes. "He's not my—"

The front door beeped and then swung open.

Penn stood in the doorway, arms laden with a bag of takeout. He was staring. She followed his gaze—her bare midriff, the curve of her waist where her cropped tee had ridden up, the frayed edge of her shorts. His throat worked.

Victoria arched a brow.

Penn inhaled sharply and jerked his gaze back to hers, cheeks darkening.

"V? Is someone there?" Clara's voice crackled through the phone.

Penn mouthed *Sorry* and turned hastily toward the kitchen, but Victoria smirked. "Clara, hold on."

She reached for the hem of her shirt, pulling it down just enough to cover most of her skin. Of course, being a crop top, it sprang right back up.

Victoria watched with secret amusement as Penn hurried toward the kitchen, his ears burning crimson. She let him get halfway before calling out.

"Penn."

He halted like he'd been shocked, shoulders rigid.

Victoria grinned. "Come meet my sister."

Penn turned slowly, one hand gripping the takeout bag so tight the paper crinkled. His Adam's apple bobbed as he swallowed.

Clara's voice shrieked through the phone. "Who is Penn?"

Victoria held the phone away from her ear, laughing. "Clara, calm down—"

"Oh my god! You have a guy there. Is it the billionaire? Does he have a big dick?"

Penn's eyes widened. The tips of his ears were now the color of ripe cherries.

Victoria sighed. "I regret everything."

Clara must've been bouncing on the other end, the sound of her chair squeaking frantically. "Put him on! Put him on right now! I'm switching to video call, hold on."

Penn took a step back, shaking his head in pure panic.

Victoria bit her lip, trying not to laugh at how flustered he was—this man who hacked government databases before breakfast. She crooked a finger, beckoning him as she accepted the video call with her other hand.

Penn exhaled sharply and walked over, his expression murderous, but he dutifully bent down when Victoria tilted the phone toward him.

Clara sucked in a dramatic gasp. "Oh, he's cute. Hi, billionaire!"

Penn opened his mouth. Closed it. Glanced desperately at Victoria.

"Clara, behave," Victoria warned, but her voice was warm.

Penn cleared his throat. "Hi."

"Are you fucking my sister?"

"Clara!" Victoria shrieked at the same time Penn choked on air.

"Uh. I brought lunch?"

Clara cackled. "Oh my god, you're adorable. Are you this awkward all the time?"

Penn blinked.

Victoria took pity on him. "Clara's into gaming," she offered. "She has strong opinions about *Elden Ring*."

Penn's gaze snapped to hers, like she'd tossed him a lifeline. "Oh." His shoulders relaxed slightly. "What build?"

Victoria watched with idle amusement as Clara launched into a rant about *Elden Ring*. Penn's shoulders loosened visibly now that they'd found neutral ground—tech and games.

"I'm a strength build," he admitted, running a hand through his hair and taking a seat on the floor next to Victoria. She handed him the phone, and he only hesitated for a second before taking it.

Clara gasped. "So you enjoy brute force cheating then?"

Penn cracked his first genuine grin. "What, and your bleed spam build isn't cheating?"

Victoria rolled her eyes as they devolved into heated gameplay debate. Clara was practically vibrating through the screen, gesturing wildly.

"You," Clara declared, jabbing a finger toward the camera, "are tragically wasted on my sister. Ditch her and marry me. I'm funnier, and I won't judge your trash builds."

Penn's gaze flicked to Victoria, that unreadable intensity back in his eyes. "Can't." He shrugged. "Your sister's scarier than Malenia, and I think she'd kill me."

Clara cackled, and Victoria shrugged. "Probably, considering she's under eighteen and it's *illegal*," Victoria said, emphasizing the last word.

Her sister giggled again. "I'm only kidding. Mostly." Her voice softened. "Okay, Penn the nerdy billionaire, you passed the vibe check. Keep my sister safe."

Penn met Victoria's gaze only inches apart. "I will."

Clara sighed wistfully. "Ugh, and he does the protective thing too. V, don't screw this up."

Victoria rolled her eyes. "Love you too, demon child."

Penn hesitated, then murmured, "Uh. We should game sometime."

Clara's answering squeal nearly shattered the phone speakers.

Victoria hung up before her sister could traumatize Penn further.

"Your sister is nice. Are you… are you hungry?" Penn scratched the back of his neck, suddenly awkward again. "I should—lunch is getting cold."

Victoria smirked. "You did well."

Penn's lips twitched. He set the takeout bag on the coffee table, unpacking containers while keeping Sandy at bay. "Objectively."

She leaned in, just a little. "No. Fact. She likes you."

His fingers stilled on the lid of the container. His exhale was audible. "And you?"

"I like you too." Victoria left him like that—flustered, frozen—and sauntered toward the table, grinning the whole way.

With the takeout containers spread between them, Penn pulled out his chopsticks, splitting them apart.

She speared a piece of shrimp fried rice with her fork. "Clara's never gonna let me live this down, you know."

Penn glanced up. "Live what down?"

"The fact that you exist."

He huffed out a near-silent laugh, shaking his head. "I'm not that interesting."

Victoria smirked. "You hacked the FBI, built your own surveillance empire, and somehow managed to endear yourself to my sister in under two minutes. You're definitely interesting."

Penn's chopsticks stilled. He didn't look up this time, feigning deep interest in the container between them. "I was afraid she'd remember me from the few times I went over to your house all those years ago."

The shift in tone caught Victoria off guard. She studied the curve of his jaw, the way his fingers tightened faintly around the chopsticks. "Clara was a toddler. And I haven't told her or my mom that you're from…before. She just knows you now—and now she thinks you're cool."

He let out a slow breath. "Good. I guess it helps that she thinks I'm a billionaire with a big dick." The grin he shot her was mischievous.

Victoria choked on her rice, and Penn handed her a sparkling water while he laughed at her. "She…she came up with that on her own."

"Even the billionaire part?"

"Yes," Victoria said, nodding. "I have my guesses, but I'm old enough to know not to ask about either of those things."

"You mean money and dick size?"

Laughing, Victoria nodded.

"Well, she's right," he paused and shrugged. "At least about the first thing. As for the second…" His words trailed off and he glanced down at his crotch. "It's technically above average, at least according to a quick Google search."

"You've looked up the average penis size?" Victoria couldn't stop the grin that crossed her face.

"What man hasn't?" He returned her grin.

"God, this is such a weird conversation."

"Want me to save it?"

Sandy nosed her way between them, sniffing at Penn's knee. Without hesitation, he slipped her a piece of chicken under the table.

"Please do. I've got nothing."

Penn cleared his throat. "Well, if you're not tired of it yet… I was thinking you could come back to the lab with me today. There's more I want to show you. About the case."

"Yeah," Victoria said easily. "I'd like that."

———

WHEN THEY REACHED HIS WAREHOUSE—HIS SANCTUARY, as he called it—Penn parked and killed the engine. He didn't move right away, just sat there, staring at the steering wheel. Victoria waited, giving him the space to gather his thoughts.

Finally, he exhaled and opened his door. "Let's go."

The warehouse was exactly as she remembered it—a world of screens, wires, and blinking lights. Penn moved through the space like he belonged there, his fingers brushing against keyboards and monitors as if they were extensions of himself. Victoria followed, her attention darting from one piece of tech to the next, trying to make sense of it all.

"This is still insane," she murmured, more to herself than to him.

Penn glanced over his shoulder, a faint smile tugging at his lips. "I'll take that as a compliment."

He gestured to a couch, and she sat, watching as he pulled up a series of windows on one of the larger screens. Her father's face appeared, followed by a cascade of documents and photos.

"I've been going through everything I could find on your father's case," Penn said, his voice steady now, focused. "There's not much that hasn't been scrubbed or redacted, but I managed to piece together a few things."

Victoria leaned forward, her eyes scanning the screen. "Like what?"

"Like the fact that your father was presiding over some seriously big cases. Mafia linked cases. Drug cartel cases. Even some human trafficking cases." Penn tapped a few keys, pulling up a list of names. "These are the people he was judge over. Most of them are untouchable—politicians, corporate executives, people with enough money and power to make problems disappear."

Victoria's stomach churned. "And you think one of them is behind this?"

"It's possible." Penn hesitated, then added, "But it's taking time to search through all the databases I have access to."

Victoria glanced at the computer screen, her father's case files still glowing in pixelated lines and blocks of text. Penn's hands were busy on the keyboard, his focus razor-sharp as he initiated another test. The soft hum of the machines filled the room.

"What can we do while it runs?" she asked, her voice breaking through the silence.

Penn glanced up and pushed his glasses up the bridge of his nose. He shrugged, a faint crease forming between his brows. "Nothing, really. Not unless you've got a knack for cracking encryption."

She shook her head, a small smile tugging at her lips. "Can't say I do."

"I guess... I guess we could talk while these run. If you want."

"That would be nice."

Penn stood then, hesitated for a moment, and walked over to sit beside her on the worn leather couch. "So," he started. "You've been in witness protection for over a decade. What's that like?"

Victoria let out a breath, leaning back into the couch. "Lonely. Always looking over your shoulder. Always pretending to be someone you're not." She turned to him, her gaze searching his face. "At least when I'm on stage, I want to be someone else. But with WITSEC, I just... Sometimes I just want to be me."

"You, as in Vanessa?"

"I don't know anymore. I suppose I'm a twisted hybrid of both now." Before he could ask a follow-up question, she spoke.

"What about you? Living in this... fortress and working at Crest Strategies. Is it what you thought you'd be doing now?"

Penn frowned, his fingers tapping against his thigh. "It's... controlled. Predictable. I know what's coming in here. Out there—" He gestured vaguely toward the warehouse doors. "Out there, it's chaos. I can't control chaos."

"But you try," she breathed, her eyes lingering on his face. "You control what you can. That's why you watch. Why you protect."

He met her gaze then, and his expression shifted to something more unguarded. "Yeah," he admitted. "I guess I do."

The distance between them seemed to shrink without either of them moving. Victoria's breath caught, her pulse quickening as Penn's gaze dropped to her lips. His hand twitched, as if he wanted to reach for her but wasn't sure if he should.

She decided for him, leaning in just enough to bridge the gap. Their lips met. The tentative brush sent a spark through her veins.

Penn froze for a heartbeat, then his hand came up to cradle her face, his touch warm and surprisingly gentle.

The first kiss was soft, hesitant—a question more than a statement. Victoria barely had time to register the warmth of Penn's lips before he pulled back, his breath uneven, his hazel eyes searching hers for permission.

She didn't give him words.

Her fingers curled into the front of his shirt, dragging him back in. This time, there was no hesitation. Penn's mouth crashed against hers, his long fingers sliding into her hair, tilting her head to deepen the kiss. A low sound escaped him—something between a groan and a sigh—and Victoria answered it with one of her own, her body arching into his.

Penn's hands dropped to her waist, gripping hard as he hauled her onto his lap. The sudden shift made her gasp, but he swallowed the sound, his tongue sweeping against hers in a rhythm that sent heat spiraling through her. She could feel him—all of him—the hard press of his arousal against her center, the way his fingers dug into her hips.

Victoria rocked against him, a slow, deliberate grind that dragged a ragged curse from his lips. Penn's grip tightened, his breath coming in short, harsh bursts against her mouth. "Fuck, Ness—"

Her breath hitched as Penn's hands slid beneath her shirt, his fingers rough and warm against her skin. The kiss turned feverish—his mouth demanding, teeth grazing her lower lip before he sucked it between his own. She arched into him, pressing her breasts into his palms, and a low groan rumbled in his chest.

His touch was electric as he slipped beneath her bra, calloused fingers rolling her nipples until they peaked, sending sharp sparks of pleasure straight to her core. She rocked against him, the friction of her jeans against his erection drawing a broken sound from his throat. He shifted on hand back to her hips, guiding her movements, grinding her down harder.

"Penn—" His name escaped from her lips, half plea, half demand.

He answered by dragging his mouth down her neck, teeth scraping over her pulse. "Tell me," he whispered, breathless, against her skin, fingers digging into her flesh. "Tell me what you want."

She didn't get the chance.

A sharp, insistent *beep* cut through the haze of desire. Penn stilled, his breath ragged against her collarbone. The sound repeated—louder, more urgent.

"Fuck." Penn froze, his forehead dropping against hers as he exhaled hard. "Shit. I've got to go restart the test again."

She didn't want to let him go. But he was already pulling back, his hands reluctantly leaving her body as he crawled out from under her. He strode toward the monitors, adjusting his glasses as he went.

Victoria watched as he dragged a hand through his disheveled hair, his fingers flying across the keyboard to silence the alert. The screen flickered, data streaming too fast for her to follow—until it stopped.

Penn went still.

His voice was low, disbelieving. "What the fuck? That makes no sense."

CHAPTER EIGHT

PENN

PENN'S FINGERS FROZE OVER THE KEYBOARD.

Detective Albert Morrison.

The name glared back at him from the screen, red-flagged in his facial recognition feed. His stomach dropped. The cop who had been assigned to protect the Jordan family after the hit on Judge Gary Jordan. The same cop who, according to the records Penn had just cross-referenced, had ties to a string of human-trafficking rings that were shut down and the perpetrators brought to court in Victoria's father's last major case. Not only that, he'd gone missing after someone ratted him out, and was seen near the crime scenes of every jury member death from that case.

Penn's jaw clenched.

This wasn't just a stalker. This was a cleaner. Someone who had been erasing loose ends for years. Or maybe it was revenge for putting the human trafficking rings out of business.

A sharp inhale from behind him. Penn twisted in his chair just in time to see Victoria's face drain of color.

"The detective?" Her voice was barely audible. "He's the man who pulled me into the alley?"

"Just because we got a match doesn't mean he's the one who did it." Penn said, even though it absolutely made sense.

He swallowed hard and turned back to the screen, pulling up Morrison's recent movements—traffic cams, financials, anything that could give them an edge. That in itself was difficult because of the man's disappearance. But after a few minutes of tense silence, something came up.

A ping from a security camera near a high school.

The image was captured over an hour earlier, and Morrison's wasn't the only face Penn recognized.

"Is that... oh fuck, Clara!" Victoria gripped Penn's arm in a tight grip, her eyes going wide. "He's after my sister." Victoria disappeared from his side, already on her phone. She left the control room, and in his security cameras, Penn watched her for a second as she started pacing up and down the hallway, one hand in her hair, the other holding the phone.

Shit.

Penn grabbed his own phone. He tried Briggs first—no answer. Tanner next—straight to voicemail. His gut twisted as he shot emergency alerts to local patrol units near the high school, praying to a god he didn't believe in that they'd get there in time. But he knew they wouldn't. The image was from an hour ago.

They were too late.

Victoria reappeared in the doorway, her phone clutched in a white-knuckled grip. Her face was ghostly.

"My mom—" Her voice cracked. "She went to pick Clara up, but a man told the office he was Clara's father. He took her. Oh god, she's gone!"

Penn's throat closed.

Victoria's breath came in short, sharp bursts, her fingers trembling as she shoved her phone at him. The screen showed unanswered calls to Clara's phone. No response. Nothing. Victoria swayed on her feet.

Penn was moving before he could think. His hand caught her elbow, steadying her as she sagged against him. A choked sob escaped her, and he pulled her in without hesitation, one arm wrapping tight around her shoulders while his other hand still clutched his phone, firing off another urgent message to the team.

"Clara's smart," he murmured against her hair, his voice rough but steady. "She'll find a way to call, or signal, or—"

Victoria's fingers curled into his shirt, her body shaking against his. "I can't lose her, Penn."

His chest ached.

He tightened his grip, pressing his lips to the crown of her head before he could stop himself. "You won't."

Penn held Victoria as she shook against him, her tears soaking into his shirt. She fell apart in his arms. He knew he should say something —anything—but words had never been his strength. So he just held her, his fingertips tracing slow circles against her spine as she buried her face in his shoulder.

"We should get you back to the safe house," he murmured after a long moment.

Victoria shook her head violently, fingers tightening in the fabric of his shirt. "N-no. I can't be alone right now."

Penn hesitated. His pulse hammered in his throat, but he forced the words out. "You can... stay with me. If you want."

Victoria lifted her head, her eyes red-rimmed as they searched his face. "With you?"

He swallowed. "Yeah." He gestured vaguely toward the exit. "We'll get Sandy, whatever you need, but—yeah, you can stay with me. Unless you don't want to. But I agree, you shouldn't be by yourself. I could send Jenna or—"

"I'll go with you." Victoria exhaled shakily and nodded, pressing back into him for just a second before pulling away.

They swung by the safe house first. Victoria packed an overnight bag in jerky, mechanical movements while Sandy, sensing her distress, pressed against her legs. Penn waited by the door, fidgeting with a receipt from lunch that was folded in his pocket.

It was only when they were pulling away that Victoria spoke again.

"Where do you live?"

Penn tightened his grip on the wheel. "West Village." A pause. "It's, uh. Pretty basic."

Victoria let out a watery, disbelieving laugh. "Penn. You're a tech billionaire. Nothing about you is basic."

His cheeks burned. "I didn't mean—"

"I know," she murmured.

He didn't look at her.

His penthouse was, objectively, excessive—three floors of sleek, minimalist space with floor-to-ceiling windows overlooking Manhattan. But Victoria didn't comment on the view as Penn let them inside. Her gaze skimmed the walls lined with framed vintage video game posters, the half-disassembled server humming softly in the corner of the living room, the worn-in couch with blankets tangled haphazardly over the back.

Penn cleared his throat. "Guest room's down the hall." He pointed. "Fresh sheets. Towels in the bathroom. Uh. My room's next door if you—"

Victoria's fingers brushed his arm, cutting him off. He stiffened at the contact.

"Thank you," she whispered.

Penn couldn't hold her gaze. He nodded and stepped back, letting his hand drop from Sandy's leash. The dog trotted after Victoria as she moved toward the hallway, overnight bag slung over her shoulder.

He didn't exhale until the guest room door clicked shut.

Then he sank onto the couch, rubbing his hands over his face. His phone buzzed in his pocket—Briggs, finally checking in. But for the first time in years, he didn't immediately scramble for answers.

Instead, he stared at the closed door down the hall and wondered how the hell he was going to get Clara back. Because he had to get her back—for Victoria.

———

PENN PACED THE LENGTH OF HIS HOME OFFICE FOR THE third time in ten minutes, the glow from his eight monitors casting long shadows across the floor. He drained the last of his energy drink and crushed the can between his palms before tossing it into the recycling bin. It landed with a hollow clatter atop the pile already there.

His fingers moved across keyboards, pulling up every database, every dark web forum, anything that might give him a breadcrumb toward Morrison's location. More importantly, Clara's location.

The man had walked into a high school—a goddamn high school—and strolled right out with Clara under some bullshit pretense. No wonder there were so many fucking school shootings. Security footage showed nothing. The trail ended at a dead-end street where Morrison's rental car had vanished into traffic. Penn had done more work than the police, managing to track the car until it went into a parking garage and disappeared. He'd likely switched cars, and it was impossible to know which one he'd left in.

Penn snarled and slammed his palm against the desk. The monitor flickered but stayed upright.

Think.

He minimized his current screen and opened a new browser, typing furiously. Clara's Steam ID popped up—he'd pulled her gaming profiles weeks ago when Victoria first agreed to protection. He knew long before talking to Clara on Victoria's phone that her sister was a gamer. And it wasn't just *Elden Ring*. The kid played an MMO called *Eclipsis* religiously. His fingers hesitated over the keys for half a second before he logged in under a dummy account, mimicking the language of a teenage gamer.

Anyone seen StarK1tten online? he typed into the guild chat. *We were supposed to raid.*

Three dots appeared immediately.

Dude, she was on yesterday, typed a user called XxShadowWolfxX. *Said she'd be on tonight, but I haven't seen her.*

The dots vanished. Penn waited. Another message popped up.

Hello?

Penn leaned closer, fingers hovering.

A new username chimed in.

Who's this?

Penn hesitated.

Old friend, he typed. *Just checking in.*

Another pause. Then—

dude ur mic is on, someone crying in the background?

Penn ripped the headset off. The soft, broken sound of sobbing reached him instantly.

Victoria.

He closed out of the game and knocked over his chair scrambling to get up. After nearly tripping over the tangle of charging cables under his desk, Penn bolted toward the hallway, his pulse hammering in his throat.

The guest room door stood slightly ajar. Penn shoved it open the rest of the way, expecting to find Victoria curled up in bed. But the room was empty. The comforter was smooth, untouched minus the shaggy dog lying at the end of the bed.

"Where is she, Sandy?" Penn asked.

The dog just gave him a sad look at the same time the sound of running water cut through the quiet.

The ensuite bathroom door was closed, mist seeping from beneath it. "Victoria?" Penn rapped his knuckles against the wood.

No answer—just a muffled gasp and another choked sob.

His stomach lurched.

"Victoria, I—are you okay?" Silence. He swallowed hard, fingertips pressing into the doorframe. "I'm coming in." Penn didn't hesitate. He slammed his foot against the door just below the lock—once, twice—until the wood splintered and swung inward on broken hinges.

Steam choked the bathroom, the mirror fogged over, the tiles slick with condensation. The scalding water still poured down over Victoria, where she crouched on the tile floor, arms wrapped around her knees. Her skin glowed an angry red, raw from the heat, but she didn't flinch—just rocked slightly, breaths hitching between stifled sobs. She didn't react to the crash of the door, didn't even lift her head. Just sat there, shaking, tears lost in the spray.

Penn's breath seized. Shit. She was naked.

He went for the shower knob, his own breath catching as superheated water seared his forearm. He hissed—the pain barely registered past the vice grip clamping around his chest—and wrenched the knob hard to the left. The water sputtered off, leaving only the oppressive hiss of steam and Victoria's shuddering breaths.

She didn't move. Didn't look up. Just sat there trembling, arms locked around her knees, skin flushed red from the scalding spray.

Penn didn't think. He stepped into the shower—still in his jeans—snatching the towel from the nearby rack on his way in. The fabric barely stretched wide enough, but he draped it over her shoulders anyway, shielding her body from view. Only then did he risk glancing at her face.

"Ness." His voice cracked.

She didn't react. Just pressed her forehead harder against her knees, fingers digging into her shins.

Penn hesitated, then sat fully on the wet floor beside her, heedless of his clothes. He tugged the towel tighter around her before sliding an arm beneath her knees, the other around her back, and pulled her sideways into his chest.

Victoria went rigid for a heartbeat, then collapsed against him with a sob. Her fists twisted in his shirt, her forehead pressing into his collarbone.

Penn exhaled, his grip tightening. She was burning up, her skin still radiating unnatural heat. His fingers touched the side of her neck lightly, checking her pulse. Too fast. Too erratic.

"You gotta breathe," he muttered, rubbing his palm in slow circles between her shoulder blades. "Come on. In and out."

She shook her head violently, fingers digging into his ribs.

"Clara—"

"I know," Penn cut in. His voice was coarse, barely controlled. "I know. But she's smart. She's tough." He dared to press his lips to the top of her damp head. "And she's yours. Which means Morrison just signed his own death warrant."

Victoria shuddered against him, her breath hitching. Penn could feel the moment her spine gave out, the way her whole body sagged under the weight of exhaustion and terror. He adjusted his hold, pulling her more securely into his lap.

"I got you," he murmured. His thumb traced the ridge of her cheekbone. "I'm not losing either of you."

She didn't answer. But her fingers unclenched, her cheek resting against his chest. Penn stayed motionless, counting every unsteady rise and fall of her ribs.

Over her shoulder, through the broken door, Sandy jumped down from the bed and trotted over, curling up against Penn's side. Her wet nose nudged Victoria's limp hand, drawing a shuddering sigh from her. Victoria didn't move, but her hand shifted, tangling in Sandy's fur. The dog whined, licking her wrist.

Penn exhaled and rubbed slow circles between Victoria's shoulder blades, damp through the thin towel. His pulse pounded in his own ears—too loud, too frantic. He should be moving, hacking, hunting. But the weight in his arms anchored him.

Sandy settled her head on Victoria's thigh, ears flat. The silence stretched.

No alarms. No calls. Just the three of them, waiting.

CHAPTER NINE

VICTORIA

VICTORIA WOKE TO UNFAMILIAR SHEETS AGAINST HER BARE skin. For one blissful, disoriented second, she didn't remember. Then her memories slammed into her—Detective Morrison, the photo from Clara's high school, Clara not answering her phone, the shower, the scalding water, the way her own skin had burned but she hadn't cared because her sister was missing.

Then—Penn.

Penn carrying her, towel-wrapped and shaking, to this bed. Penn's voice low in her ear. *Not losing either of you.*

She curled onto her side, pressing the heels of her palms against her eyes. The ache behind her ribs was unbearable. *Clara, Clara, Clara*—

But beneath the terror was something else, something that made her stomach tighten with a different kind of heat. The memory of Penn's hands on her. The way he hadn't hesitated to break the door down to get to her. The way he'd sat with her. Held her. Let her shatter against him.

Her face burned because all the while, she'd been naked.

With a sharp exhale, she sat up, peeling back the covers. The towel lay crumbled beside her, as if he'd put her to bed in it. Knowing him, he probably had. She found her clothes folded on the nightstand—the same sweatpants and t-shirt she'd packed from the safe house. Victoria dragged a hand through her tangled hair before pulling them on.

The penthouse was quiet except for the hum of electronics—screens, servers, whatever else Penn had wired into his walls. She followed the sound of movement toward the kitchen, bare feet soundless on the hardwood.

She paused in the doorway.

Penn leaned against the counter, laptop open on the island, fingers flying over the keys. Shirtless. His grey sweatpants hung low on his hips, and the morning light caught the sharp angles of his collarbones, the taut lines of his abdomen. He wasn't bulky, but lean and toned, the kind of body built more by restlessness and pacing than weights. His glasses sat slightly askew, lenses reflecting lines of code, and his hair stuck up in disheveled tufts, like he'd spent the night running his hands through it.

A pan of eggs sizzled beside him, mostly ignored.

Victoria's breath caught.

He focused on something on the laptop, then turned—no hesitation, no delay, like he'd known she was there. His gaze locked onto hers.

"You're up."

"I'm up."

"Are you hungry? I'm making—oh shit." He spun, diving for the spatula to move the eggs around the sizzling pan. "Damnit. I lost interest. I was making eggs. They may be be a little…crispy."

"You cook." The words came out before she could think.

He huffed, scratching the back of his neck. "Barely. Microwave eggs are tragic, though."

Penn cleared his throat and turned back to the laptop, talking fast —too fast, like he was afraid of the silence. "I dug deeper while you slept. Clara's friends said she got into a dark sedan—tinted windows, no plates. I matched it to traffic cams, tracked it heading west until it vanished in a parking garage off Seventh. Briggs sent her team to sweep it. Car was there, wiped clean." A muscle in his jaw flexed. "No Clara."

Victoria's stomach dropped.

He kept going—slinging the partially charred eggs onto a plate, still talking, words rapid-fire. "I backtracked Morrison's known associates, dug through his financials. He's got a pattern. Favors three safe houses—"

Victoria moved before she realized she was going to.

She crossed the kitchen in three steps and wrapped her arms around him from behind, pressing her face between his shoulder blades. His skin was warm under her cheek, his heartbeat a quick, steady thud against her palm.

Penn went completely still.

"Um, I'm not done yet," he muttered after a second.

Victoria squeezed tighter. "I know."

He turned in her grip with the plate in one hand, eyebrows furrowed, searching her face. "Then why—?"

"Because you're here. Because you're trying to help find my sister. And you made me eggs."

"They-they're burned." His breath stuttered. His free hand hovered at her hips like he wasn't sure where to put it.

Victoria rose onto her toes and kissed him.

The plate of half-burnt eggs clattered onto the counter behind him, forgotten. Penn made a noise against her mouth—half surprise, half hunger—before his hands found her waist, fingers pressing into the soft curve of her hips. Victoria curled her fingers into his hair, tugging just enough to tilt his head back, and kissed him harder.

His lips parted under hers, breath hot and uneven. "Ness—"

She nipped his lower lip. "Say it again."

"Ness." His voice cracked.

She'd never heard her name sound like that—like a prayer, like a curse, like something he'd been holding onto for years.

His hands slid up her sides, thumbs brushing the underside of her breasts through the thin cotton of her shirt. She arched into the touch, and he groaned, fingers flexing like he wanted to memorize the shape of her.

"I thought about this," he muttered against her mouth. "Every goddamn night for years. It was worse after I found you again."

She pulled back just enough to see his face—flushed, pupils blown, lips red from her teeth. "Prove it."

Penn didn't hesitate. He spun her, pressing her back against the counter, and dropped to his knees.

Victoria's breath hitched.

His hands slid down her thighs, pushing the sweatpants down her hips. "You're sure?"

She tangled her fingers in his hair. "Yes."

He exhaled, shaky, and pressed his mouth to the inside of her thigh. His teeth grazed skin, just shy of pain, and she shuddered.

"Penn."

He looked up at her, glasses askew, lips parted. "Yeah?"

"Birth control's covered, and I'm clean."

A flicker of relief crossed his face. "Me too. But—" His grip tightened. "This isn't because you feel like you owe me, right? Or because you're scared? Or you need some sort of... distraction? Because I can give you a distraction, but I don't want you regretting this later. If you want, I can wait. I'll always wait."

Victoria cupped his face, thumb brushing his cheekbone. "I want you. Not because you saved me. Not because you're helping me. Because you're you."

He made a broken sound and dragged her pants the rest of the way off. Without hesitation, he lifted her right leg and tossed it over his shoulder. Victoria leaned back against the counter, using a mixture of it and him to keep herself upright as she wobbled on one leg.

The first swipe of his tongue had her gasping, one hand tightening in his hair. He licked into her like he was mapping her. Learning her.

"Fuck," she breathed.

Penn hummed against her, the vibration sending a shock of pleasure up her spine. His hands gripped her hips, holding her still as he worked her over with his mouth—licking, sucking, teasing until her thighs trembled.

Victoria's breath hitched. He tormented her, lapping at her clit in a way that made her hips jerk forward instinctively. He chuckled against her, the sound low in a way that sent a shiver racing down her spine.

"You're impatient," he murmured, his breath hot against her skin.

"You're—" She broke off with a gasp as his tongue circled her clit again. "Fuck, Penn." Not once had she ever imagined him like this—so confident, so in control—and it was driving her wild.

He suddenly pulled back, his hands leaving her long enough to peel off his glasses. He tossed them onto the counter beside her with a careless flick of his wrist, and her stomach flipped. Without the glasses, his eyes were darker, more intense, and they locked onto hers as he leaned in again, his breath fanning over her damp skin.

"Still with me?" he asked, his voice rough.

She nodded, her throat too tight to speak. He smirked, his lips curving wickedly, and then he was on her again. He licked into her like he was trying to devour her, and she bit down on her lip to stifle a moan. Her hips rolled against his face, seeking more friction, more pressure, or at least something to fill her, but he held her still, his grip firm.

"Fuck, Penn," she gasped, her nails digging into his scalp. Maybe she was hurting him, but she couldn't bring herself to care as the man on his knees drove her to insanity.

He chuckled against her; the vibrations sending shocks of pleasure through her, and then he slipped a finger inside her, curling it just right. Her back arched off the counter, a sharp cry escaping her lips. He added a second finger, stretching her, filling her, and she rocked against his hand, chasing the sensation.

"You're so much better than I ever imagined," he muttered against her, his voice muffled but no less intense. "So fucking perfect."

The words sent a thrill through her. Her thighs trembled around his shoulders, her breath coming in short, uneven gasps. He quickened the pace of his fingers, hitting that spot inside her that made her vision blur, and his tongue worked her clit in relentless circles.

"I'm—" She broke off with a strangled moan, her hips jerking erratically. "Penn, I'm—"

"I know," he growled, his breath hot against her.

Her thighs clenched around his head as the wave crashed over her, her body shuddering. She rode his face and fingers, her moans echoing off the walls, until the pleasure ebbed, leaving her trembling and boneless against the counter.

Penn didn't stop until she pushed him away—gently, but insistently. He knelt there for a second, breathing hard, before he stood and pressed a kiss to her hip, his lips soft against her skin. His hands lingered on her thighs, thumbs stroking over the sensitive skin on the inside, and she shivered.

She tugged at his hair. "Up. Now."

He rose, lips glistening, and she slid her hand down the waistband of his sweatpants. Her fingertips brushed hot, velvety skin. She didn't hesitate. With a tug, she dropped his sweatpants, and his cock sprang free. When she wrapped her fingers around him, his breath punched out in a choked gasp.

Oh.

Her brain stalled for a second—not just because of the size, though Jesus Christ, she wasn't complaining—but because of the way he felt. Hard under her palm, his pulse jumping against her fingers. She'd imagined this a dozen sleepless nights lately, but reality was hotter, heavier, better.

She tightened her grip and dragged her fist up slowly—just once.

"Ness—" His hips jerked, fingers digging into the counter behind her. His voice fractured on her name, rough-edged and wrecked.

She smiled and did it again.

Penn swore, head dropping forward, shoulders taut. Three strokes and he was trembling, his breath ragged.

Good.

Victoria let her thumb swipe over the wetness at the tip, smearing it slowly.

He made a noise like his spine was dissolving. Penn hissed, hips jerking. "Christ, Ness—"

Victoria's breath hitched as Penn's hand wrapped around hers, stilling her stroke. His wild dark eyes locked onto hers, and for a moment, she thought he might pull away. Instead, he spun her, pressing her back against the counter again, and dropped to his knees.

"Again?" she gasped, her voice breaking.

"Not yet." His lips curved into a smirk that made her stomach flip. He hooked his hands under her knees and pulled, sliding her away from the counter and dropping down until her back hit the cold tile floor. The shock of it against her bare skin made her yelp, but Penn was already on her, his weight pressing her into the floor as his mouth claimed hers.

This wasn't the awkward boy she'd known in high school. This was a man who knew exactly what he wanted—and he wanted her.

His kiss was bruising, all teeth and tongue, and she arched into him, her hands clawing at his back. His skin was hot under her palms, the muscles taut and shifting as he moved. She could feel him against her thigh, and the ache between her legs pulsed with every press of his hips.

"Penn," she breathed, her voice ragged. "I need—"

"I know." He nipped at her lower lip, his breath hot against her skin. "But I'm not rushing this. Not with you."

His hand slid between them, fingers teasing her entrance. She was already wet from her first orgasm. It was obvious. Her body fucking wanted him, and he groaned as he pushed two fingers inside her.

"Jesus, Ness," he muttered, his voice rough. "Fuck." He drew out the word.

Victoria's head fell back, a moan tearing from her throat as he crooked his fingers, the heel of his palm grinding against her clit. He worked her in a way that left her gasping.

"Penn—" Her voice broke, her hips rolling against his hand as she choked on air. "Please."

He withdrew his fingers, and she nearly cried out at the loss. But then he was there, his cock nudging against her, and she wrapped her legs around his hips, pulling him closer.

"Look at me," he demanded, his voice hoarse.

Her gaze snapped to his, and the intensity there stole her breath. He held her there for a moment, his eyes searching hers, before he pushed into her. The stretch was exquisite, her body welcoming him like it had been made for him, and she dug her nails into his shoulders, her head falling back again.

Penn caught her chin, forcing her to look at him. "Eyes on me, Ness."

She obeyed, her breath hitching as he bottomed out, their hips flush. He stayed there for a moment, his chest heaving, his eyes locked onto hers, before he pulled back and thrust into her again. Perfect. He was fucking perfect.

The rhythm was unhurried, each stroke hitting deep. Victoria's nails scraped down his back, leaving red trails in their wake. He was everywhere. His weight pressing her into the floor, his breath hot against her neck, his cock filling her in a way that made her forget everything but him.

"You feel so good," he ground out, his hips snapping against hers. "Too fucking good. Fuck."

Victoria's back arched, her hands fisting in his hair. "Harder."

He obliged, his pace quickening, the sound of skin against skin filling the kitchen. The tile was cold and unforgiving beneath her, but she didn't care—not when Penn was inside her, his eyes locked onto hers like she was the only thing that mattered.

His hand slipped between them, his thumb circling her clit, and her breath caught, her body tightening around him. "Penn—"

"Ladies first, Ness," he said, kissing her neck, sucking on the skin there until there was certain to be a bruise tomorrow. "You finish and I'll follow."

She clawed at his shoulders, her thighs shaking around his waist. His cock dragged just right inside her—long, deep strokes that lit her nerves on fire—but his thumb circling her clit was maddening. Slow, torturous circles while his hips moved faster.

She was going to lose her fucking mind.

"Penn—"

"Look at me." His fingers twisted in her hair, forcing her gaze up.

His pupils were blown, lips parted, sweat dampening his forehead. "Tell me whose."

She arched into his touch, panting. "Whose?"

His teeth flashed—so unlike the man who fidgeted and stuttered compliments. "Mine."

A bolt of heat lanced through her.

His thumb pressed harder. "Say it."

She couldn't—wouldn't—give him the satisfaction. But her body betrayed her, hips chasing his fingers as tension coiled tighter.

Penn smirked and slowed his strokes.

"Asshole," she choked.

He laughed against her mouth, breath hot. "Say it, or I stop."

Victoria bit her lip hard enough to taste copper. "You wouldn't."

He did. In fact, he pulled all the way out and stared down at her, caging her in from above. His heavy dick rested on her lower stomach, still covered in their wetness. "Say. It."

"Fuck it, Penn. You're *killing* me," she growled, nails digging into his skin.

His fingers traced slow patterns up her ribs, pushing her shirt higher. "Say it, Ness."

She exhaled sharply. "Fine. Yours. Happy? Now fuck me."

Penn smirked, leaning down to press an open-mouthed kiss to the swell of her breast. "Ecstatic." His tongue flicked over her nipple before his teeth closed gently around it, sucking until she arched off the floor with a gasp.

"Penn—" Her protest dissolved into a moan as his mouth moved to the other breast, tongue circling lazily. She swore, squeezing her thighs around his waist. "You got what you wanted, now fucking—"

He ignored her, working her skin with lips and teeth until she was writhing. Her hands tangled in his hair, tugging hard enough to sting, but he only groaned against her, his breath hot and damp. Distracted by the pull of his mouth, she barely registered the shift of his hips—until he slammed back into her with one brutal thrust.

Victoria screamed.

His dick filled her so completely her vision whited out for a second. She clawed at his shoulders, her back bowing off the tile as he snapped his hips forward again, burying himself to the hilt.

"You begged," Penn rasped against her throat, voice ragged. "I delivered."

Then he ruined her.

His pace was relentless, each thrust driving the air from her lungs. The slap of skin echoed off the kitchen walls, mixed with her choked gasps and his rough, whispered praises.

Victoria could barely think. Every nerve burned, every stroke ratcheting the tension in her stomach tighter. His fingers found her clit again, circling in time with his thrusts, and she sobbed, her thighs shaking around him.

Penn's rhythm faltered, his control slipping. His grip on her hip tightened hard enough to bruise as he fucked her through her climax, his groan vibrating against her collarbone.

Then he pulled out just in time, spilling hot stripes across her stomach with a broken curse.

For a moment, the only sounds were their staggered breaths. Penn slumped over her, forehead pressed to her shoulder, lips brushing her skin.

Victoria trailed a hand down his spine, sticky with sweat. She traced the sharp line of his jaw, and he kissed the inside of her palm. "Find my sister, Levine, and we can do that again with my vibrator."

Penn's expression darkened as he pressed another kiss to her hand. "Deal."

CHAPTER TEN

PENN

PENN'S FINGERS HOVERED OVER THE KEYBOARD, USELESS. The monitors around him displayed useless traffic feeds, dead-end surveillance stills, and looping footage of Clara's abduction—evidence that never changed no matter how many times he scoured it. His coffee had gone cold hours ago, forgotten beside an untouched sandwich Carson's fiancée Kinsley had dropped off with a pointed look.

Two days. Forty-eight hours of red tape, false leads, and police who moved too slow.

His eyes burned from lack of sleep, his skull throbbing behind his temples. Every failed search scraped raw against his nerves. He'd hacked DMVs, tapped into private security grids, even risked pinging burner phones—nothing. Clara was gone without a goddamn trace.

A knock sounded at his door.

Penn didn't turn. "Not now."

Benedict stepped inside anyway, crisp in his usual suit, ice-blue eyes scanning the chaos of Penn's workspace. "Carson wants those videos for the governor's rehabilitation campaign."

Penn dragged a hand down his face. "Later."

"He needs them today."

"Does it look like I fucking care?" Penn snarled, shoving back from his desk hard enough to send his chair rolling across the floor. The rare curse seemed to catch his friend off guard. Benedict blinked, processing.

Penn didn't apologize.

Benedict's jaw tightened, but pity edged into his gaze. "Sleep. Shower. Then—"

The office door burst open.

Victoria stood there, breathless, Jenna Briggs at her shoulder. Her hair was pulled back in a messy ponytail, dark circles bruised under her eyes. Penn barely had time to prepare himself before she crashed into him, arms locking around his chest so tight he nearly staggered. Her whole body trembled.

Penn's hands found her waist instinctively, grounding her against him. "What happened?"

Victoria didn't speak. Just pressed her face into his shoulder, fingers digging into his back.

Jenna stepped forward, handing Penn Victoria's phone. The screen displayed an open text—no sender ID, no traceable number. Just an image.

Clara.

Bound to a chair, wrists raw and bleeding. A split lip. A purple bruise blooming across her temple. Blood streaked her cheekbone, staining the collar of her ripped sweater.

Penn's vision tunneled, his lungs locking tight. He snatched the phone and stalked to his main terminal, already plugging it in, pulling up software older than Clara herself. Algorithms spun to life across multiple screens as he dumped the image into every forensic program he had.

Benedict moved closer. "Tell me what—"

"Out." Penn didn't glance up. "All of you. Now. Except her."

Jenna hesitated, but Benedict caught her arm, murmuring something. They disappeared, sealing the door shut behind them.

Victoria stayed. Silent tears tracked down her cheeks as she watched him work, her arms wrapped around herself like she might collapse if she didn't hold tight.

Penn's hands flew over the keys. He dissected the image pixel by pixel—background shadows, acoustic paneling, a sliver of ductwork visible in the corner. Warehouse? Basement? His programs scanned for GPS remnants hidden in the metadata, running facial recognition on Clara's battered face just in case the bruises altered her profile enough to fool older systems.

Nothing pinged yet.

Victoria's breath hitched—a quiet, shattered sound. Penn abandoned his chair and pulled her into him before he'd decided to move. She buried her face against his chest again, her tears dampening his shirt. Cradling the back of her head, he threaded through her hair, and pressed his lips to her temple.

"We'll find her."

Victoria shook against him. "He didn't—" She choked, fingers twisting in his shirt. "He didn't ask for anything."

Penn stiffened. No ransom. No demands. Just violence without motive. That was worse.

A soft chime came from his terminal. He turned, half-dragging Victoria with him, scanning the screens—

—background analysis flagged something. Concrete walls. Industrial-grade insulation. Patterns in the dust. His program cross-referenced urban blueprints, narrowing it to unfinished construction zones within a thirty-mile radius. Too many possible matches.

Penn grabbed his keyboard. "I need to narrow these down." His fingers flew, hacking into construction permits, contractor schedules. "I just need to—"

Victoria clutched his wrist, stopping him mid-keystroke. Her eyes were wide, frantic.

"They won't." He twisted his hand to lace his fingers through hers. "And we won't go in until we know your sister is safe."

Victoria searched his face—for hesitation, for doubt, he wasn't sure —but Penn didn't blink. Slowly, Victoria nodded. Penn lifted her knuckles to his mouth and pressed a silent vow against her skin.

PENN'S EYES BURNED. THE GLOW OF HIS MONITORS ETCHED static ghosts across his vision—blueprints of unfinished construction sites, municipal permit records, transportation logs. He'd been awake for almost forty-eight hours straight, cycling through every algorithm, every database, every thread that might pull Clara back from the dark.

Sandy had resigned herself to Penn's insomnia, flopped at his feet like a living weighted blanket. Her ears perked, and she let out a low, questioning *whuff* and lifted her head. She stared at the door.

Penn's hand drifted toward the .38 in his desk drawer.

But Sandy's tail thumped once. Twice.

A shadow moved in the doorway.

Victoria leaned against the frame, her hoodie sleeves swallowing her hands, her hair a messy tumble from restless attempts at sleep. Dark smudges bruised under her eyes. "You ever planning on shutting down?"

Penn relaxed, flexing his stiff fingers. "Can't."

She arched an eyebrow. "Not won't? Can't?"

If he stopped searching, Clara stayed missing. If he blinked too long, his brain conjured the bruises on her face, her split lip weeping blood. So instead of answering, he angled his chair toward Victoria. "You should go lie down."

"I did. Three times." She rubbed her arms, gaze flickering over the screens. "Kept seeing her every time I closed my eyes."

Penn swallowed. He understood.

Victoria drifted closer, bare feet silent on the hardwood. She paused behind him, studying the maps and data streams glowing across his monitors. Her fingers grazed his shoulder. "You really think we'll find her?"

He considered lying—but this was Victoria—his Vanessa. She deserved the truth, even if it tore. "I don't know."

Her breath stopped.

Penn twisted in his seat, catching her wrist before she could retreat. Her pulse jumped under his thumb. He pulled her gently toward him, nudging his knees wider. "Here."

Victoria hesitated, then sank onto his thighs, her weight warm and solid. She fit against him like she'd been made for the space—curve of her ass pressing into him, her back molded to his chest. Penn hesitated, then locked his arms around her waist.

She exhaled, sinking deeper into him.

For a while, they just stayed like that. Her breathing resumed and steadied. Sandy heaved a doggy sigh, resting her chin on Penn's foot. The slow rhythm of Victoria's pulse in her wrist soothed something jagged in Penn.

She turned her head, her lips brushing the hinge of his jaw. "You don't have to do this alone."

Penn huffed, tipping his forehead against her temple. "I'm the one with a private satellite uplink."

She twisted in his lap, catching his face between her palms. "You know what I mean."

His throat tightened. He did.

One of her thumbs traced the hollow under his eye. "You're going to collapse."

He caught her wrist, pressing his lips to her pulse point. "Don't care."

Victoria's mouth curled—not quite a smile, but close. "You're a disaster."

"Then it's good you're here to mitigate the fallout."

She laughed—a soft, startled sound—and something in his chest cracked open. Before he could overthink it, Penn kissed her.

Victoria melted into it. Her hands wrapped around his neck, her ass adjusting on his lap. He groaned against her mouth, pulling her tighter. The heat of her, the slick drag of her tongue, the way her back arched when he bit her lip—he forgot the exhaustion, the fear, everything except how good it felt to have her in his arms.

Then Sandy nudged his leg, whining.

Victoria laughed again, breathless. "She's judging us."

Penn scraped his teeth down her throat. "Unacceptable." He lifted her in one smooth motion—ignoring the dog's offended *boof*—and carried her down the hall to his bedroom.

The lock clicked behind them, Sandy on one side, them on the other.

Penn set Victoria down on the edge of his bed, then stepped back, giving her space to breathe, to turn him away if she wanted. His body was already ahead of his brain, blood rushing south, his pulse hammering at his throat. But he locked himself down, let his hands hang loose at his sides. Waited.

Victoria tipped her head up at him, reading his hesitation the way she always did. "You're not going to ask me if I'm sure, are you?"

He exhaled, half-laugh. "You know me too well."

She caught his belt loop and tugged. "Ask."

Penn braced a hand on the mattress beside her hip, leaning just close enough to make her breath hitch. "Are you sure? This isn't just—"

"A distraction?" She arched into him, fingers sliding up his chest, and God, the way she looked at him—like he wasn't the same wreck of a man who'd barely slept in days. "I know what I'm asking for."

His thumb traced the seam of her lips. "I don't want you to regret this tomorrow."

She nipped at him, just enough to sting. "I will never regret you."

Penn kissed her before he could ruin the moment—before he could overthink—and this time, he didn't hold back. His tongue slid against hers in a claiming way, his hands framing her face. Victoria gasped into his mouth, nails digging into his shoulders as she arched against him.

Penn dragged his lips down her throat, his teeth scraping along her pulse. "Tell me what you want."

"Jesus, Penn—" Her head fell back. "Touch me."

He didn't need specifics. He knew her body even after only one time together—the way she trembled when he palmed her, the little noise she made when he pressed his thumb just there. He slid his hand between her thighs, grinding the heel of his palm against her, and she moaned, back bowing off the bed.

"Still good?" he murmured against her collarbone.

She grabbed a fistful of his shirt. "Stop talking."

He smirked, working her slow and teasing until her hips rocked into his touch, chasing the friction. "You sure?"

"Fuck you—"

He kissed her again, swallowing her curse, and then she was pulling at his clothes, fingers frantic. Penn let her wrestle his shirt over his head, but when she reached for his belt, he caught her wrist. "Patience."

Victoria glared. "You're evil."

"And you're impatient." He dragged her hoodie up, exposing her stomach, the soft curve of her waist. He let his hands map her as he kissed a slow trail down her body—navel, ribcage, the swell of her breasts just barely covered by her thin bralette. The fabric dampened under his mouth where her nipples pebbled under his breath.

Penn dragged his tongue along the lace, then bit down. Victoria gasped, fingers twining in his hair. He didn't rush, just worked her with his mouth until she squirmed, whining low in her throat.

"Are you wet for me?" Penn murmured against her skin.

She dug her heel into his back. "Fuck, yes, and I swear to god, if you don't—"

He hooked his fingers in her waistband and yanked.

Victoria yelped as her leggings and underwear came off in one sharp tug. Then Penn was spreading her thighs, dragging her closer to the edge of the mattress, and she didn't have time to protest before his mouth was on her.

"Shit—" Her hips jerked, but Penn pinned her in place with a forearm across her stomach, his other hand pressing into the crease of her thigh to hold her open. He licked into her, slow and deep, then circled her clit with the flat of his tongue, watching her face as she shuddered. He'd missed out on the details the first time after he'd removed his glasses. Maybe he'd keep them on this time, just so he could see her reactions with clear vision.

Victoria's fist twisted in the sheets. Her breath came in short, sharp bursts. "Penn—"

He pulled back just enough to blow cool air over her, making her whimper. "Yes?"

She kicked weakly at his back. "Don't tease."

He grinned, then licked a slow stripe up her folds before sucking her clit between his lips. Victoria nearly choked, her whole body tightening, thighs clamping around his head as she came with a bitten-off cry.

Penn didn't let up, just gentled the pressure until she was writhing, oversensitive, pushing at his shoulders. Only then did he pull away, licking his lips.

Her chest heaved. She blinked up at him like she'd forgotten how to speak.

"Breathe," he reminded her.

She grabbed his face and kissed him, tasting herself on his tongue, and then her hands were on his belt again. This time, he didn't stop her.

Penn toed off his Pokemon slippers while she unbuckled him, shoving his jeans and boxers down just far enough. She wrapped her hand around his cock, and his vision hazed. He gritted his teeth as she stroked him, her thumb swiping over the head.

He caught her wrist again. "You want me to fuck you, right?"

"Yeah."

"Then stop with the hand job and lie the fuck down."

Victoria smirked. "Yes, sir."

He groaned. "Christ, Ness—"

She lifted her hips, pressing against him, and Penn didn't have the willpower left to protest. He positioned and pushed inside her, swallowing her gasp with a kiss, the tight, wet heat of her clamping around him like a vise. Fuck, she took him so well.

Penn stilled for a second, forehead touching hers, both of them breathing hard. Then Victoria rolled her hips, and he lost control.

He fucked her slow at first, deep and deliberate, until she dug her nails into his back and begged for *more, harder, yes*—and then he gave it to her. The bed creaked beneath them, his rhythm relentless, every thrust driving her higher.

Victoria's heels dug into his ass, urging him deeper. "Fuck, Penn— *there—*"

He must've hit that spot again because she came with a choked-off moan, her body locking down around him. Penn followed her over the edge, spilling into her with a groan, his hips stuttering.

For a long moment, neither of them moved. Just breath and warmth and the aftershocks trembling through them. Then Victoria exhaled, her fingers tracing lazy circles on his bare stomach.

Penn pulled out slowly and rolled onto his back beside her, one arm slung over his face. His heart still pounded, sweat cooling on his skin.

Victoria turned onto her side, propping her head up with one hand. She traced his chest with the other. "Regrets?" she murmured.

Penn cracked one eye open. "Never."

She smiled and kissed the corner of his mouth. "Good."

Sandy whined at the door.

Penn sighed. "We're being judged again."

"Well, may as well be judged for a second performance," Victoria said, rolling on top of him. "Right?"

"Fuck yes."

CHAPTER ELEVEN

VICTORIA

VICTORIA WOKE WITH THE WEIGHT OF PENN'S ARM DRAPED over her waist, his face buried against her shoulder. His breathing was deep, even—finally asleep after nearly three sleepless days searching for Clara. The tension had left his body, but his fingers still curled possessively into the sheet near her hip, like even unconscious, he refused to let go.

She slipped out from under him carefully, pressing a kiss to his temple when he made a soft noise of protest. His lashes fluttered, but exhaustion kept him under.

Good. He needed rest.

She showered quickly, washing away the scent of sweat and sex. The water turned scalding as her thoughts circled back to Clara—her sister's terrified face in that photo, the bruises dark against her pale skin. Victoria had spent half the night lying awake in Penn's arms, clawing through every memory, every hint, anything that could lead to where Morrison had taken her.

When she returned to the bedroom, Penn hadn't moved. Still buck naked, sprawled across the mattress, one hand outstretched where she'd been, like his body refused to accept she wasn't there anymore.

She grabbed her phone from the nightstand and padded barefoot into the living room. The dim glow of Penn's monitors bathed the space in flickering blue. Sandy lifted her head from the couch, thumping her tail once before settling back down.

A new message notification from an unknown number glared at her from the lock screen.

> 5th and Mercer. You have one hour. Or I start sending her back to you in pieces.

Victoria's breath left her in a sharp rush. Her fingers trembled as she swiped to the attached image—Clara, gagged, wrists bound with zip ties, a fresh bruise under her eye. And behind her, chains against a cement wall.

Her pulse pounded in her throat.

"Fuck," she whispered.

She dressed in silence—jeans, boots, the pocketknife she always carried tucked into her waistband. The apartment was still dark, barely dawn. If she left now, she could beat Morrison's deadline.

A floorboard creaked behind her.

Victoria turned.

Penn stood in the doorway, rumpled and half-awake, his glasses perched crookedly on his nose. His hair stuck up at odd angles where he'd slept on it. But his eyes—sharp, alert—locked onto hers like he could already see the plan forming in her head.

"Where are you going?" His voice was rough with sleep, but there was nothing sleepy about the way his gaze flicked to the phone still clutched in her hand.

Victoria tucked it behind her back. "Out."

Penn's jaw tightened. He stepped forward, fingers threading through his hair to push it out of his face. "Don't lie to me."

"I'm not."

"Bullshit." He closed the distance between them in three strides, hand snapping out to grab her wrist. With a sharp twist, he flipped her palm up—her phone screen still lit, Morrison's threat glaring between them.

Penn's breath hitched. His grip tightened. "No."

"I have to." She tried to pull free, but he yanked her closer.

"Like hell you do." His free hand cupped her jaw, forcing her to look at him. "You walk into that meeting, you don't walk out. You know that."

"I can't just—"

"You can." His thumb brushed her cheek. "Because I can find her. Let me work. Let me fix this."

Victoria's chest ached. She wanted to believe him. But Clara's face in that photo—

She curled her fingers into his shirt. "Penn—"

He kissed her. Not gentle, not soft—a hard, desperate press of his lips. His grip on her jaw tightened, keeping her still as if he could convince her through sheer force.

Victoria let herself sink into it for three heartbeats, then pulled back. "Okay."

Penn exhaled, forehead dropping to hers. "Okay?"

"I'll wait." She smoothed her hands over his chest, feeling the rabbit-quick thud of his heart. "Just—just give me a second."

She kissed him again, slower this time, letting her body relax against his.

Penn sighed into her mouth, tension bleeding out of his shoulders. When he finally pulled away, his lips were slightly swollen, his glasses crooked again.

"I just need five minutes," he muttered, scrubbing a hand over his face. "Then I'm going to figure this out."

She nodded. Watched him stagger back toward the bedroom.

The moment the door clicked shut, she moved.

———

VICTORIA'S BOOTS CRUNCHED OVER GRAVEL AS SHE approached the meeting spot—an abandoned industrial lot surrounded by rusting chain-link fences. She glanced over her shoulder, her pulse quickening. No sign of Morrison. Yet.

No sooner had she thought it than a shadow moved to her left. She froze, hand instinctively going to the pocketknife in her waistband.

"You're early." The voice was feminine—familiar in a way that made Victoria's skin crawl. Jenna Briggs stepped into the light, her auburn braid slung over one shoulder, her narrowed gaze scanning Victoria with a mix of irritation and relief.

Victoria's stomach dropped. "Jenna. What the hell are you doing here?"

"Levine called me." Jenna's strode towards Victoria as she pulled out her phone, her tone clipped. "He's not stupid, Ms. Omstadt. He knew you'd pull something like this."

Victoria's jaw tightened. "I don't need a babysitter."

"You're right. You need a punching bag." Jenna's lips twitched faintly as she held up the phone. "But maybe save it for later. Penn's about thirty seconds from losing his mind."

Victoria glared at her as Jenna dialed. The phone didn't even ring once before Penn's breathless voice crackled through. "Jenna. Is she there?"

"She's here," Jenna said, her gaze never leaving Victoria. "Safe. For now."

"Let me talk to her."

Victoria snatched the phone from Jenna's hand, her anger flaring. "Penn, I told you I—"

"Victoria, don't," he cut her off, his voice sharp. "I'm getting in my car now. Just—" There was a thud and his voice cut out.

Before Victoria could ask what had happened, Jenna went rigid. Her posture shifted instantly, her body tensing like a coiled spring, her eyes narrowing as she stared at the phone.

"Levine? Penn? You there?" Jenna's voice was a low hiss. There was no response. "Shit. Something's wrong."

The phone cracked again, but the voice that came through wasn't Penn's. It was deeper, rougher—a voice that sent a cold wave of dread crashing over Victoria.

"Hello, Vanessa."

Her blood solidified, freezing in her veins. Morrison.

"You've been a busy girl," he continued, his tone mocking. "But time's up. I've got something new to play with now."

Victoria's grip on the phone tightened so hard her knuckles turned white. "What did you do?"

"Let's just say your little hacker friend isn't as clever as he thinks he is." Morrison's laugh was a low, cruel rumble. "No more cheating. He's mine now."

The line went dead.

Victoria's legs nearly gave out. She stared at the phone, numb, her mind racing. Penn. Morrison had Penn.

Jenna was already moving, taking her own phone out of Victoria's hand and punching in a number. Her voice was tight when she spoke. "Carson, we've got a situation. Penn's been abducted. Call a meeting with—"

Victoria cut her off. "We don't have time for a meeting."

Jenna's gaze snapped to hers. "And what's your plan? Go charging in blindly? That's how people die, Victoria."

"He has Penn!" Victoria's voice broke, the words clawing their way out of her throat. "I'm not just going to stand here while Morrison—"

"You think I don't know that?" Jenna stepped closer, her voice dropping to a low growl. "But going in without a plan isn't just suicide —it's wasting whatever time Penn has left. So, pull your shit together and let's go."

Victoria's chest heaved, her fists clenched at her sides. She forced herself to breathe, to think. Morrison had Penn. He'd taken him from somewhere—his lab, his penthouse, the car. Wherever he'd been on his way here.

"His car," she blurted, the realization hitting her like a punch. "Morrison intercepted him on the way. There's no chance he got into Penn's penthouse without triggering alarms."

Jenna nodded, already tapping something into her phone, talking to someone else. "Dani, check the parking garage at Penn's apartment. See if you can find anything. In the meantime, I have Ms. Omstadt and we're headed towards base."

94

CHAPTER TWELVE

PENN

DARKNESS SWAM BEHIND PENN'S EYELIDS WHEN consciousness first dragged him back. Pain split his skull. His thoughts were sluggish, weighed down by the thick fog of whatever had knocked him unconscious. He inhaled slowly through his nose. The air was damp, cold, tinged with mildew and the faint copper tang of blood.

His own blood, he realized, when he tried to move and fire lanced up his side.

His wrists were bound behind his back, secured with cold metal cuffs. His fingers twitched instinctively, testing their range—nothing. Restrained. Abducted. Shit.

Memory clawed its way back in jagged fragments.

Victoria sneaking out. The desperate call to Briggs. The relief when Jenna confirmed Victoria was safe.

Footsteps behind him in the parking garage. The sickening crack against his skull.

Penn forced himself to breathe through the nausea curling in his gut. He needed to assess his surroundings, figure out where Morrison had taken him, what he was dealing with. Because it had to be Morrison. Although, he supposed, it could be ill timing from someone else who knew he had access to a lot of money and friends with even more. That's why he'd built in safeguards against him being abducted.

Safeguards that clearly didn't work.

He blinked against the dim light from a single flickering bulb, trying to sharpen his vision. It didn't help that somewhere along the way, he lost his glasses. They weren't completely necessary, more for filtering out blue light more than anything, but there was a slight prescription for his near sightedness. His fuzzy gaze swept the shadows—crates stacked haphazardly, rusted tools leaning against stone walls—until his attention caught on a small figure curled in the corner.

Penn's heart stopped.

She was hunched in on herself, knees pulled tight to her chest, her light hair streaked with sweat. Clara. She looked so much like Victoria had at that age—same stubborn tilt to her chin, same sharp features. Bruises mottled her arms, her lip was split, and she wasn't moving.

Shit. Fuck.

She wasn't moving.

Penn's stomach dropped. *No, no, no.*

He twisted his wrists uselessly against the cuffs, ignoring the bite of metal into his skin. Swallowing against bile, he shifted onto his knees, dragging himself closer in awkward, shuffling motions. His ribs screamed, though he wasn't sure why. But he gritted his teeth and kept going until he was near enough to nudge Clara's shoulder with his own.

"Clara." His voice scraped, barely audible. "Hey. Wake up."

She jerked violently, gasping as she scrambled backward.

Penn instinctively leaned back, giving her space despite the way every instinct screamed at him to shield her. "It's okay. It's Penn."

Her wild gaze darted over him—torn shirt, bloodied lip—before recognition flickered in her eyes. Relief sagged her shoulders, but she didn't relax. "Y-you're—" She swallowed, coughing weakly. "You're Victoria's billionaire with the big—"

"Hi." Penn exhaled through his nose, relieved she was coherent.

"Yeah." He glanced toward the ceiling—listening for footsteps—before shuffling closer. "Morrison bring you here?"

"I don't know his name." Clara wrapped her arms tighter around herself. "I don't even know how long I've been down here." Her voice cracked. "He—he said—" She squeezed her eyes shut, shuddering.

Penn didn't press. He didn't need details to know the horrors Morrison had inflicted. Instead, he tipped his head slightly toward his bound wrists. "Anything we can use to get these off?"

Clara hesitated before shaking her head. "No."

Penn swore inwardly but nodded. "Alright. That's fine. We'll figure it out."

Clara swallowed hard, gaze flicking toward the cellar stairs. 'He wants my sister." Her whisper was barely audible. "He knows she'll come."

Penn's jaw locked. Yeah. She would. And Morrison was counting on it.

He shifted closer until his shoulder brushed Clara's lightly—grounding her, reminding her she wasn't alone. "Your sister's smart," he murmured. "And she's got a scary woman named Jenna Briggs with her."

Clara's breath hitched. "But they don't know where we are."

Penn tilted his head, catching her gaze. "They will. Trust me." He needed to keep her talking—keep her distracted from the cold cellar and Morrison's inevitable return. "You play video games, right?" he asked casually, nodding toward Clara's fingers, which were twitching restlessly.

Clara nodded

Penn inclined his head slightly. "Well, we have time to talk games, if you want."

Her shoulders relaxed marginally. "I mostly play MMOs."

"Roleplayer or min-maxer?"

Clara hesitated before admitting, "Min-maxer."

"Good girl." He grinned. "You ever touch legacy code?"

Her brow furrowed. "I—I messed around with Python."

Penn's smirk widened. "Oh, so you're dangerous, then?"

She blinked at him, startled, before the faintest ghost of a smile touched her lips.

Penn kept her talking—easy topics, dumb coding jokes, shifting carefully so she didn't see him testing his restraints again. His wrists were slick with blood now, but he ignored it, his focus split between Clara and listening for Morrison's return.

He was fully aware when the cellar doors creaked open. Penn twisted instantly, putting himself between Clara and the stairs, shielding her as footsteps descended. Morrison's silhouette emerged—broad-shouldered, looming, his face shrouded in shadow until he stepped into the dim light.

Penn had seen worse men in his lifetime. But few had eyes like Morrison's—flat, dead, like a zombie in one of the games he and Clara had just been discussing.

Morrison grinned, kicking aside an empty crate as he approached. "Well, look who's awake."

Penn didn't respond. He'd dealt with bullies before—they thrived on reaction, on fear. Silence pissed them off more than insults.

Morrison's smile flickered when Penn refused to speak. His boot lashed out without warning, catching Penn's ribs.

Pain lit up Penn's side—he gritted his teeth, absorbing the force without making a sound. Behind him, Clara stifled a whimper.

Tilting his head, Morrison sneered. "Quiet, huh?" He crouched, grabbing Penn's chin and forcing his head up. "Guess hacker-boys know how to stay invisible. But you're out of luck, Levine. I see you."

Penn remained still, unflinching.

Morrison's grin sharpened before he shoved Penn back and straightened. "Fine." He shrugged, stepping past Penn toward Clara.

Penn twisted violently, blocking Morrison's path with his body.

"Protective of the little Jordan girl too?" Morrison paused, amused. He put his hands on his hips. "You know, Vanessa was in the room when I stabbed their father. Didn't know it at the time. I sure would like to get my hands on her, though. Maybe I'll play a little first. Does she like it rough, Levine?"

Blood pounded in Penn's head, but he didn't break eye contact. He also remained silent, though everything in his head was screaming profanities at the man threatening the woman he loved. But a reaction was exactly what Morrison wanted.

The asshole chuckled before grabbing Penn's collar and hauling him upright, dragging him toward a rusted metal chair bolted to the floor in the center of the room. He threw Penn into it, and with his hands still bound behind his back, Penn struggled for balance, landing with a thud in the chair. Morrison strapped him down around the chest first before securing his ankles with straps thick enough to bind a bear.

Morrison leaned close, his breath sour against Penn's ear. "You know, I didn't realize until recently that you're worth a shitload of money."

Penn didn't react.

Morrison smirked. "How much do you think Crest Strategies will pay to get their little hacker back?" Morrison's patience started to fray when Penn remained silent. *Crack.* He backhanded Penn across the face hard enough to snap his head sideways. Metallic blood filled Penn's mouth, but he swallowed it, expressionless.

Morrison growled, slamming his fist into Penn's stomach. And again.

Penn took it—breath forced from his lungs, ribs screaming—but he refused to make a sound besides a grunt with each impact.

His ribs screamed with every shallow breath, the pain white-hot where Morrison had hit him. But Penn had learned long ago how to detach from pain, how to dissociate his consciousness from the screaming protests of his body. The cliché bullies at school had given him that skill.

Morrison paced in front of him like a predator circling its prey, occasionally glancing at Clara, who had curled herself into the corner, watching with wide, terrified eyes.

Yes. Penn had dealt with men like Morrison before. Bullies, sadists, people who got off on control. The only thing they hated more than defiance was being ignored.

Morrison's fingers tightened, his nails sinking into Penn's shoulders from where he stood behind him. "Oh, you're going to be difficult, huh? That's fine. I got time." He released Penn, strolling toward Clara, who whimpered.

Penn's muscles twitched, but he stayed still. *Keep his attention.* If Morrison kept talking to him, kept hitting Penn, Clara stayed safe.

Morrison crouched in front of Clara, tilting his head as if studying a specimen under glass. "You know, you look just like your sister," he murmured. Clara flinched as he touched a strand of her hair, twirling it between his fingers.

Penn's heartbeat pulsed in his ears. If the asshole was going to hurt her...

Morrison smirked, glancing back at Penn. "You got a type, Levine? I guess she's a little young for you, huh?"

Penn clenched his jaw but remained silent.

Morrison laughed low, standing and walking back to Penn. "Come on, man. You think I don't know what you are? Some freak who got rich playing with computers? You think you're some kind of protector now? Keeping Vanessa from me. Trying to act all tough for her sister. Funny." His boot pressed down on Penn's bound foot, grinding slowly. Pain shot up his leg, but Penn barely flinched.

Morrison's expression darkened. He leaned in, lowering his voice. "Tell you what," he murmured, "I'll make you a deal. You tell me where Vanessa is, right now—and I'll let you play with her sister."

Penn's vision tunneled. A red haze of fury crept at the edges of his awareness, but he forced it back down. He couldn't lose control—not when Clara needed him to stay sharp.

He finally spoke, his voice quiet, measured. "I may be a computer freak, but I practically live on the dark web. And when I get free, Morrison, I will make sure you die screaming for mercy in the most twisted illegal ways possible."

Morrison blinked. Then he howled with laughter, slapping his thigh. "Oh shit! There it is! The little hacker's got a spine after all!" He wiped mock tears from his eyes before his expression hardened into something truly monstrous.

"I was gonna take it easy on you," Morrison mused, cracking his knuckles. "But now? Let's see how tough you really are."

Penn didn't flinch as Morrison's fist connected again.

The *crack* of bone echoed in the cellar. Pain splintered through Penn's face, his skin splitting under the force. His head snapped to the side, blood dripping from his lip. He worked his jaw, swallowed the copper taste, and stared back up at Morrison, refusing to look away.

Morrison grinned. "Perfect."

Another blow. Then another.

Each strike was meant to break him. But Penn had spent his life hiding pain, surviving it. He didn't cry out. He didn't beg. He just sat there, stealing glances at Clara, making sure she was still breathing, still unharmed.

And that seemed to infuriate Morrison more than anything.

"You think you're protecting her by letting me beat your fucking face in?" Morrison sneered, wiping Penn's blood off his knuckles. "Let me tell you something, Levine. Once I finish with you, I'm gonna take my time with her. Make her scream like her sister did after I gutted her old man."

With a groan, Penn rolled his head to the side and spit out blood. "Try. Harder. Bitch."

CHAPTER THIRTEEN

VICTORIA

VICTORIA PACED. THE POLISHED FLOOR OF CREST Strategies' conference room reflected her distorted shadow—back and forth, back and forth—past the sleek wooden table where the men argued. Their voices blended into meaningless noise beneath the hammering of her own pulse.

Penn's gone.

Had been gone for twenty-three hours and fifty-six minutes. She clenched her fists, nails digging half-moons into her palms. Her skin felt too tight, her lungs shallow. Across the room, Jenna Briggs leaned against the wall, arms crossed, watching her with sharp eyes. Waiting.

"—tracking software should have picked up something by now—"

"—he had to have expected this—"

Victoria exhaled sharply, tipping her head back toward the ceiling. The overhead lights blurred her vision.

They were right about that. Penn had to have expected this. Not because of her, but because of his standing. His money. He had to have left a way to find him.

Her gaze flicked to Tanner Whitney, fists braced against the table as he snarled something at Benedict. Broad shoulders tense beneath his dark shirt. The sleeves were rolled up, revealing scars and ink. The others were polished—Benedict in a tailored suit, Carson Crest with his immaculate posture, James Rothschild wearing a tie and a vest—but Tanner looked like he'd walked straight out of a battlefield. At least he'd probably be useful when they found Penn.

If they found him.

Victoria swallowed. Her mind snapped into focus, cutting through the noise. She cleared her throat. The room didn't stop. She tried again, louder. Silence fell. Five sets of eyes fixed on her.

"I need him found," she said. No waver. No hesitation.

Carson straightened. "We're working on—"

"No." Victoria stepped forward. "You're arguing. Penn needs action."

Jenna pushed off the wall. "While I appreciate the fire, we don't even know—"

Four sharp alerts cut through the silence in unison. Carson, Benedict, James, and Tanner all stiffened, pulling their phones from pockets in eerie synchronization. Victoria's pulse hammered against her ribs as Tanner flipped his screen toward the others.

It was an alert with Penn's face on it.

A map flashed on the display. A blinking red circle pulsing far north of the city, deep in rural farmlands. Benedict's knuckles whitened around his phone. "This says he set a dead man's switch. If he didn't manually cancel it every twenty-four hours…"

"He's telling us where to go," James finished, voice low.

Victoria didn't wait. She snatched the nearest phone—Benedict's—and zoomed in. A range of coordinates. A timestamp. She shoved it back at him. "You have vehicles? Gear?"

Tanner was already moving toward the door. "Armory's downstairs."

"No." Jenna stepped in front of him, blocking his path. "We go quiet. If Morrison has backup, or if he's expecting a full assault…"

"She's right." Victoria exhaled sharply. "Morrison doesn't want Crest Strategies. He wants me. I'm your bargaining chip. He took Penn because he knew I'd come for my sister and for Penn. So that's the play."

Carson's gaze sharpened. "You're suggesting bait."

"Yes," Victoria shrugged. Her fingers curled into her palms. "I'm an actress. All I have to do is play the part he wants me to play. He'll take me to Clara and Penn."

"How do you know?" Jenna asked.

"He wants to hurt me. The best way to do that is through them. Once I have eyes on them, I'll send a signal and you can come in." Victoria took a deep breath.

Jenna tilted her head. "You're assuming he won't just kill you on the spot."

"That's a pretty fucking reckless assumption," Tanner spat.

"He could've killed me in that alleyway. He didn't." Victoria folded her arms.

The instant Benedict opened his mouth to protest, she cut him off with a sharp slice of her hand through the air.

"I'm telling you, he's playing with me. He didn't kill Clara when he took her—he sent a photo. He wants me to react." She met Tanner's glare head-on. "And you charging in there with a gun just gives him exactly what he expects, and takes away his game. Hell, that's why he took Penn. He said we'd been cheating. Penn wasn't playing the game the way Morrison wanted, what with all of his protection around me. By taking Penn, Morrison thinks he's evened the playing field."

"He has," Benedict muttered under his breath. Then louder, "By taking Penn, he's seriously crippled us."

"But look," Victoria gestured towards their phones. "Penn left a cheat code. A way to take back the advantage. We can't overlook this."

Carson leaned back in his chair, fingers steepled. "So you think Morrison wants you to walk in there alone."

"He wants me terrified. Begging. Helpless. Just like my father was when Morrison killed him." The bitter words spilled out. "If I give him that, he'll take me where Penn and Clara are—because that's part of his game. Breaking me in front of them or them in front of me. Maybe both. Fuck, it's probably both."

A muscle flicked in Jenna's jaw. "Or he could just shoot you the second he sees you."

"He is more of a knife person, from what Penn and I found." Victoria shook her head. "Besides, why drag it out? He had years to kill me if that's all he wanted. He's clearly been stalking me for a while." She pushed her sleeves up, bracing her hands on the table. "The fact is, I'm going in there for my sister and for Penn."

Tanner exhaled hard through his nose, shaking his head. "I don't like it, Omstadt."

"I don't care," Victoria shot back. "Penn is in trouble because of me. I owe him this."

Carson stared at her, his lips thinned, the harsh fluorescent lights emphasizing the rigid set of his jaw. "You don't owe Penn anything. He did this because he cares about you."

"The feeling is mutual."

A beat of silence. Then, James let out a quiet breath. "She's right." He glanced at Tanner and Jenna, then back at Victoria. "If Morrison wants her to play the helpless victim, that's exactly what she should give him. Only—" His eyes darkened. "It won't all be an act."

Victoria swallowed. She'd be helpless. Genuinely helpless. Walking in with no weapon, no defense, no way to fight back until she was sure Clara and Penn were safe.

Jenna exhaled through her teeth. "You'd be unarmed. Alone. Against a dangerous man who clearly has no problem hurting people. And you'd have to sell that helplessness like your life depends on it."

"I can do it." Victoria lifted her chin. "I'm good at performing under pressure. That's literally my job."

Tanner folded his massive arms. "Even if you get to your sister and Levine, there's no guarantee you'll have an opening to signal us."

"So I make one. Those coordinates—if I'm there, if Morrison lets me see them, I need to know you'll move fast."

Jenna nodded. "We won't be far."

Carson drummed his fingers once on the table. "And if Morrison decides to cut his losses and just slit your throat the moment he gets close enough?"

"Then I'm sure as fuck taking him down with me."

The last farmhouse sat at the edge of the coordinates Penn's emergency signal had given them. It was an old, weather-beaten structure flanked by overgrown fields and rusted equipment. Shadows deepened as dusk settled, stretching long across the dirt road Victoria walked alone.

Her skin prickled beneath the cheap, oversized hoodie Jenna had scrounged up; something to make her look small, vulnerable. Perfect prey. Her hands trembled, but not just for show. She hadn't lied to Crest's team. Acting terrified wasn't hard when every instinct screamed at her to run.

She glanced over her shoulder once, but Tanner and Jenna were already ghosts. They'd peeled off when the road narrowed, trusting her the rest of the way.

Alone now.

The farmhouse loomed ahead, its cracked windows reflecting the dying light like hollow eyes. A crow cawed nearby. Silence followed. Victoria exhaled, rubbing her arms like she was cold; just an anxious girl lost on back roads, looking for shelter. Waiting.

A twig snapped behind her.

Her pulse spiked, but she didn't spin around. Play scared, not prepared. She quickened her steps, letting her breath hitch.

"Vanessa." Morrison sung out her real name in three eerie syllables. "Now what are you doing out here all alone?"

She froze, making herself turn slowly.

He stood six feet away, thumbs hooked lazily in his belt loops. No weapon in sight, but his posture screamed confidence. Like he'd already won. She hoped he was wrong. Really fucking hoped.

"I-I don't—" She bit her lip, shrinking into the hoodie. "Where— Where is my sister? Where's did you take Penn?"

His lips peeled back in a grin. "Aw, are you out here looking for them? That's cute." His gaze flicked past her, surveying the empty road. Testing. "Where's your watchdog?"

Victoria feigned confusion, taking a step back. "W-who?"

Morrison stepped closer, studying her face. She let her knees wobble.

"I know you didn't walk all the way out here. So, where are they? Are they waiting for a signal from you?" His grin sharpened when her breath hitched. "How far away are they? Do you think they'll be fast enough to save you?"

Victoria took another step back, trying to keep the same distance between them, but he kept closing it. "Just tell me where they are."

"That's my line, little actress." He lunged suddenly, snapping a hand around her wrist. She gasped, muscles locking. Everything she'd ever been taught in WITSEC and self-defense classes flashed through her mind. Though he was stronger, she was sure she could get out of the hold. But she didn't. Instead, she pulled away from him, trying to get away like the average terrified woman would.

"Help, somebody hel—" He wrapped a hand around her mouth, and her heartbeat thundered in her ear.

Morrison exhaled, satisfied. "Yeah. That's what I thought." He yanked her forward, forcing her to stumble beside him toward the farmhouse. "Let's go reunite you with your loved ones."

Victoria let him drag her, questioning if she'd made the biggest mistake of her life.

CHAPTER FOURTEEN

PENN

PENN LET HIS HEAD FALL BACK AGAINST THE DAMP CELLAR wall, the cold seeping through his shirt. The cuffs bit into his wrists, but he kept his expression neutral. Clara's shallow breaths echoed beside him. She'd curled into herself, bruised knees drawn to her chest. Fifteen years old. Fifteen, and shaking like a lamb in a slaughterhouse.

"You still with me?" Penn's voice came out ragged, but he forced it lighter.

Clara lifted her chin. A cut on her lip had crusted over. "I told you not to ask me that every five minutes."

A corner of his mouth twitched. Kid had steel in her. Just like her sister.

Morrison hadn't returned for hours. The bastard had left them in the dark—literally—with nothing but the flickering bulb overhead casting skeletal shadows. Penn had counted the passing minutes by the steady drip of water somewhere in the cellar. His ribs screamed, his face throbbed, his vision blurred at the edges, but he focused on the girl.

"You ever play *Stardust Horizon?*" he asked.

Clara blinked at him. "The RPG?"

"Yeah. I programmed a mod for it. Added an entire dungeon just for kicks."

Her eyes flickered with interest before dimming. "Pretty sure we're already in a dungeon."

Penn huffed a laugh that cost him. Something sharp twisted in his side. "Fair point." He shifted, wincing, to face her better. "But here's the thing about dungeons. They've always got an exit. You just have to find the right switch."

Clara's fingers curled into her jeans. "Or hack the game."

"That," Penn said, grinning despite the blood in his mouth, "is exactly the right answer."

Clara picked at a loose thread on her sleeve. "Do you think—" She swallowed. "Do you think my sister's looking for us?"

Penn stilled. Victoria's face flashed in his mind—those fierce eyes, the way she'd looked at him like he wasn't invisible to her.

"Yeah," he said, softer. "She is. She's saved my life before."

Clara's fingers stilled on the thread. "What do you mean, she saved your life?"

Penn exhaled through his mouth, his broken nose too clogged to allow him to breathe properly. The words stuck in his throat, but the kid deserved to know. "I knew your sister before. Back when she was Vanessa."

Clara's head snapped up. "What?"

"I was a sophomore. She was a junior." He shifted, the cuffs clinking. "I'd been tossed from foster family to foster family, and often, that came with a new school and new bullies. I... I'm not good at talking to people. Never have been. And I understood things faster than most kids. It made me a target at every school I went to. Didn't matter how hard I tried to fit in. There were always bullies waiting to beat me up." He coughed, groaning as his broken ribs sent a shooting pain through his torso. "Well, I'd been at the school for a week before I decided I was done."

"Done with what?"

"Foster families. School. Bullies. Life." Penn struggled for a deep breath. "Your sister, Ness, found me on the roof of the high school. I was standing on the edge, trying to figure out if I should dive head first into the cement, or if it wouldn't really matter because it was four stories up."

"You were going to kill yourself?" Clara sounded shocked.

"Like I said, I was done. I was moments away from doing it, too. Ness walked up to the edge. She didn't scream. She didn't panic. She just... talked. Like we were sitting in a café or something. She asked me why I was up there, what had happened, and then she offered to take me downstairs so we could talk better." His lips twitched into a faint smile. "But I didn't want to go back down. I said I couldn't. And then she told me she'd stay up there with me. That she didn't care how long it took, but she wasn't going to leave me alone. If I jumped, she'd jump too." He let out a breathless laugh. "I told her it was a bad idea—that she probably had a family, a life—it was too important. She said, 'Well, then don't jump. My life is in your hands.' Honestly, it was really stupid of her, but somehow, it worked."

Clara's voice came out soft. "She always knows what to say."

"Yeah." Penn's chest tightened, not from the pain of his broken ribs but from the memory. "She's always been like that. She didn't know me then, not really. But she saw me. Really saw me. And that's the thing that changed it for me. Nobody had ever done that before. I used to be invisible."

For a moment, the cellar was silent except for the steady drip of water. Clara stared at him, her eyes gleaming. "Do you love her?"

Penn didn't hesitate. "Yes."

"How long?" she whispered.

"Since the moment we walked down off that roof." His voice cracked, and he swallowed hard. "I've loved her for a very long time. That's why I have to get out of here. Because I need to tell her. And I'm going to get you out too."

Clara's lower lip trembled, but she nodded, pressing her back against the wall. "Okay. I—"

The cellar door burst open before she could finish speaking, and Penn's world crashed down around him.

Morrison descended the rotting wooden stairs, dragging Victoria with him. The dim bulb flickered over them, casting jagged shadows. Her face was pale, a bruise forming high on her cheekbone, but her eyes burned when they locked onto Penn and Clara.

Morrison sneered, shoving Victoria forward. She stumbled, catching herself at the last second.

Penn moved, forcing his battered body between Clara and Morrison. His broken ribs screamed in protest, his vision blurring at the edges. He didn't have time to hurt.

"Look who finally decided to show up." Morrison's voice dripped with mock fondness. "Vanessa made it just in time for the show."

Penn didn't miss the way Victoria flinched at the name. She never flinched when he called her that. Fucking Morrison was corrupting it. He didn't deserve the right to call her that.

"Penn," she breathed as she took a step towards them. Her gaze darted behind him to Clara, and she reached for them. "Are you both—?"

"No touching," Morrison snapped, grabbing her arm and wrenching her back before she could take another step.

Victoria twisted in his grip. "Let go of me—"

Morrison's grip on Victoria's arm turned violent, and Penn lurched forward. His wrists burned where the cuffs bit into flesh. Clara let out a choked noise behind him.

No. No, no, no—

"Get the hell away from her." Penn growled, the words raw.

Morrison smirked and shoved Victoria hard. She hit the concrete with a gasp, palms scraping against the rough stone. Pain flickered across her face before her expression flattened into defiance.

Penn swallowed against the fury in his throat. He wanted to lunge, to tear Morrison's spine out through his goddamn ribs, but the second Clara whimpered, his focus snapped back. He angled himself tighter between her and Morrison, blocking her view.

The kid shouldn't see this.

"You ready to put on a real show?" Morrison asked, circling Victoria as she pushed herself up. "You know, I just knew you'd come running when your little watchdog got snatched."

Victoria spat blood at Morrison's boots. "Fuck you."

Penn's chest tightened. Stupid. Brave. Perfect.

"Actually, I think I'll fuck you." Morrison grabbed her hair, yanking her head back.

Penn jerked against the cuffs so hard his vision whited out. Metal cut deeper, hot blood trickling down his fingers. "Touch her again and I'll peel your skin off while you scream."

Morrison laughed and drove his knee into Victoria's stomach.

She folded with a punched-out gasp. Clara screamed.

Penn turned—chains be damned—twisting his body in front of Clara, shielding her despite the agony screaming through his ribs.

"It's okay," he gritted out, not looking back. *Christ. Make it stop.* "Don't watch."

Victoria curled on the floor, shaking, but when her eyes flicked up to Penn's, they burned. Not terror. Not surrender.

Calculating.

Morrison grabbed her again, hauling her up by her jacket. "You don't look so righteous now, bitch."

He slammed Victoria onto the cellar floor. Her teeth clacked together, a sharp gasp tearing from her throat. Penn wrenched at the cuffs—useless, useless—as Morrison straddled her, planting his knees on either side of her ribs.

"Always knew you'd come crawling back," Morrison drawled, pinning her wrists to the concrete. His fingers dug into her pulse points. "Like father, like daughter—can't resist playing with fire."

Victoria twisted, bucking under him. Her knee jerked upward—missing by inches—but Morrison barely swayed. His grin widened, mocking, as he leaned down until his breath fogged against her cheek. "Try harder, sweetheart."

Penn's vision tunneled. The chains bit deeper, metal grinding bone. *Think. Think faster.* His gaze darted—rotting beams, exposed wiring, Clara's wide, terrified eyes—anything he could use. *Nothing.*

"You were good at staying hidden," Morrison continued, shifting his weight to trap Victoria's thigh. "That is, until you stepped into

Broadway's spotlight. I doubt I would've found you except for that interview you did at the start of your career four years ago."

Penn's stomach dropped. That was when he found her too. He didn't like the idea of comparing himself to the monster leering over Victoria.

"I'd had my fun with the other jury members and their families. Yours was the last on my list, and I'd resigned myself to the idea that I might never find you again. Oh well. But then," Morrison crooned, dragging a finger down her cheek, clearly savoring her flinch. "Then I saw your pretty face and thought to myself, 'look at that. Maybe old Albie still has some luck left in him.' Now I get to finish what I started with dear old Dad. Tie up all the loose ends with a pretty little bow. I'll make sure to say hello to mommy dearest when I'm done with you two."

Penn's blood roared in his ears, drowning out Clara's hitched breaths behind him. Victoria snarled, twisting her hips to buck him off, but Morrison chuckled low and dark, pressing down harder. "Fight all you want," he murmured, dragging his nose along her jaw. "It's better that way."

Penn's vision flashed red. Clara's choked whimper broke something in Penn's chest.

He barely registered the pain in his wrists, his ribs, his face. He could only focus on the way Morrison's hand slid down Victoria's side, gripping her hip possessively. The way Victoria's breath shuddered between clenched teeth. She was still fighting, thrashing under Morrison's bulk.

Morrison chuckled, fingers skimming the waistband of her jeans. "Knew you'd be a fighter. Just like your sister."

Penn's vision tunneled. Every ragged breath sent fire through his ribs, but the pain was nothing compared to the sight of Morrison's hands on Victoria—his fingers digging into her skin, his weight pinning her down.

His Victoria. *His* Ness. *His*.

Gritting his teeth, Penn heaved himself up, ignoring the scream of his body. His legs shook, but he locked his knees. Morrison didn't notice. Too busy leaning down, his lips brushing Victoria's ear as he whispered something that made her flinch.

Penn lunged.

He didn't have his hands, didn't have a weapon—just his body, his weight, his fury. He rammed his shoulder into Morrison's side, knocking him off Victoria with a grunt. They crashed to the floor in a tangle of limbs, Penn's momentum carrying them both onto the damp concrete.

Morrison snarled, twisting beneath him. "You little shit."

A fist cracked into Penn's jaw. White light exploded behind his eyes. Another punch landed, then another, each one a hammer blow to his already broken face. Blood filled his mouth again.

But Morrison wasn't getting back to Victoria.

Penn rolled, taking the next punch on his temple, his vision swimming. He couldn't fight back, not with his hands cuffed behind him, but he could be a goddamn obstacle. And, fuck, he was good at that.

Morrison grabbed Penn's hair, slamming his head into the floor. "You think you're saving her?" he hissed. "You're just delaying the inevitable."

Penn spat blood into his face.

Morrison reared back, fist raised.

A leather strap snapped tight around the asshole's throat.

Victoria yanked, her arms trembling, her teeth bared in a snarl. The belt, one from the chair, bit into Morrison's neck, cutting off his air. His hands flew up, clawing at the noose, his face purpling. She didn't loosen her grip. Victoria dragged Morrison backward, her muscles straining, until his thrashing slowed, his eyes rolling. Only when his body went limp did she let him slump to the floor.

Then she was on her knees beside Penn, her fingers shaking as they brushed his cheek. "Are you—?"

"Keys," Penn rasped. "Pocket."

She patted down Morrison's body until she found the keys. Her breath was heavy as she fumbled with them. The cuffs finally clicked open, and Penn let out a sigh of relief.

"Thank fuck," he choked, struggling to sit up and wrap his arms around her. She apologized when she squeezed him too tightly, and he smoothed her hair down with one hand. "Help your sister," he wheezed.

Victoria scrambled to Clara, unlocking her cuffs. The second the metal fell away, Clara launched herself into Victoria's arms, her face buried in her sister's shoulder.

Penn dragged himself all the way upright, his vision swimming. He reached for them, his fingers brushing Victoria's back.

She turned, her free arm hooking around his neck, pulling him into the embrace. Clara's small frame pressed between them, her body trembling.

Penn closed his eyes, his forehead resting against Victoria's. Her breath was ragged, her pulse wild under his fingertips, but she was alive. They all were.

A low groan split the air.

Victoria stiffened against him, her grip tightening. Penn's eyes snapped open just as Clara let out a sharp gasp.

Morrison stirred on the ground, his hand already closed around something. Without his glasses, it took Penn a second to realize what it was.

Shit.

Fuck.

"No!" Victoria's voice screamed, but it was too late.

Morrison's fingers closed around the trigger. His glassy eyes locked on Clara, the barrel pointed at her chest.

Penn didn't think. He moved.

Victoria lunged for Clara, her body twisting to shield her sister. Penn threw himself forward, his hand reaching for the gun.

The shot echoed in the cellar.

If it was possible, more searing pain exploded in Penn's chest. His breath hitched, but he didn't stop. His fingers closed around Morrison's wrist, twisting hard. The gun clattered to the floor. Penn snatched it, his vision tunneling.

Morrison's eyes widened, his mouth opening to snarl something. Penn fired twice. The first bullet ripped through Morrison's forehead, snapping his head back. The second tore through his temple before his body even hit the floor. Blood pooled beneath him.

Penn's lungs heaved as he stared down, the weight of the gun in his hand suddenly unbearable. The adrenaline that had propelled him forward ebbed, leaving a cold, hollow ache in its wake. His chest burned, the pain sharp enough to make his teeth clench.

Victoria's voice cut through the ringing in his ears. "Penn."

The gun slipped from Penn's fingers. It clattered against the concrete, but the sound felt distant, muffled under the heavy thud of his own pulse. The cellar spun like a glitching screen.

"Penn." Victoria's voice cut through the fog as she said his name again. She was searching his face, her lips parted, breath coming fast. "Are you okay?"

He nodded, or tried to. Something warm and thick slid down his ribs. "Fine," he lied. This was far from fucking fine. Everything fucking hurt.

When he tried to stand, his knees buckled. The cellar floor rushed up to meet him. His palm slapped against damp concrete to brace himself, but his arm gave out—too weak, too slow. He crumpled sideways.

Victoria lunged for him, but her fingers only grazed his sleeve. "Penn—!"

Cold seeped into his side. He blinked down at himself, at the dark stain blooming across his shirt. He pressed a hand to it, and his fingers came away slick. Red. Too much red.

"Jesus Christ." Victoria scrambled to his side, her knees hitting the floor hard. Her hands fluttered over his chest, his ribs, never quite landing. "Oh god—no, no, no—"

Clara's small cry cut through the cellar. "Is he—?"

Victoria didn't answer. She tore at Penn's shirt, buttons scattering, fabric ripping. The air hit the bullet wound, and Penn hissed through his teeth.

"Fuck," Victoria breathed. Her fingers pressed hard against the bleeding hole, trying to staunch the flow. Crimson welled between them. "Look at me. Penn, look at me."

He tried. Her face swam in and out of focus—pale skin, green eyes wide with terror. He wanted to tell her it was okay. But his tongue felt too heavy, his throat clogged with copper.

"Stay awake." Victoria's voice cracked. She shifted, ripping a strip from his shirt sleeve, twisting it into a makeshift bandage. Her hands shook as she pressed it around his chest, pressing too tight. Pain lanced through him. His gasp came out wet.

Clara hovered behind them, her arms wrapped around herself. Tears spilled down her cheeks. "We need to get out of here," she whispered. "He—he needs a hospital."

The world started to narrow to the frantic sound of Victoria's voice and the paralyzing cold creeping through his veins.

His last thought before the dark swallowed him was of her face. The way she'd looked at him on the roof all those years ago, like he wasn't something disposable. She'd made him want to live then, and she made him want to live now. This time, though, he wasn't sure it was his choice.

CHAPTER FIFTEEN

VICTORIA

THE HOSPITAL ROOM SMELLED TOO STERILE. VICTORIA pressed her thumb against the side of her index finger, worrying the skin raw. Across from her, Clara slumped in the visitor's chair, her sneakers kicking restlessly against the vinyl seat. The bruises under her eyes had darkened to a deep purple, stark against the pallor of her face.

Penn lay motionless on the bed, his chest rising slowly beneath the thin hospital gown. IV lines snaked from his arm, pale against skin usually flushed with the glow of monitors. Too still. Too quiet.

Victoria exhaled sharply and glanced at the flowers she'd brought —white peonies, arranged haphazardly in a glass vase. Too bright. Too much life for this sterile limbo. She shouldn't have—

A rasping inhale cut through the silence. Penn's fingers twitched against the sheets.

Clara jerked upright. "He's waking up."

Victoria's chair screeched as she shot forward, elbows braced on the mattress. Penn's lashes fluttered—once, twice—before his eyelids lifted halfway. Hazel eyes, unfocused but aware, locked onto her face.

His chapped lips parted. "Ness..."

Victoria's throat tightened. She reached blindly for Penn's hand—his fingers curled weakly around hers.

Penn blinked sluggishly, blinking himself into focus. Recognition flickered through his gaze. He swallowed, voice scraped raw. "Hey."

She squeezed his hand. "Hey."

Penn's mouth quirked—just enough to make her breath catch. "Knew—" His voice broke. He cleared his throat, wincing. "Knew you'd save me a-again."

Victoria let out a chuckle laced with tears. "As cliché as it sounds, I think this time, we saved each other."

"You're right," Penn nodded once, wincing. "It's hella c-cliché."

Victoria's fingers tightened around Penn's hand, grounding herself in the warmth of his skin.

Clara hovered at the edge of the bed, her arms crossed tightly over her chest. "You scared the crap out of us, you know. Next time, maybe don't jump in front of a gun. Just a thought. You don't get a second life like in a game."

Penn's lips twitched, the ghost of a smirk. "Noted," he rasped, his voice still rough. He shifted slightly, wrinkling his nose as the movement tugged at the bandages across his chest. "How long...?"

"Two days," Victoria answered before he could finish the question. She brushed her thumb over the back of his hand, her gaze flicking to the monitors beeping steadily beside the bed. "They had to... stabilize you. Lost a lot of blood."

He nodded. "Morrison?"

"Dead. You made sure of that."

"I hope he's b-burning in hell." Penn exhaled, a slow, shaky breath. His eyes slid shut for a moment, then opened again, focusing on Clara. "You okay, k-kid?"

Clara rolled her eyes, but her bravado faltered. "I'm fine. Mostly. Thanks to you." She hesitated, then added, "And, uh... thanks for, you know, not dying."

"Anytime. You're tougher than you look, Clara. D-didn't need me."

"Yeah, I did," Clara muttered. Her cheeks flushed, and she looked away.

Penn's gaze flicked past her shoulder, a sudden stillness in his expression. His fingers flexed weakly against hers before his thumb brushed the inside of her wrist—hesitant, questioning.

She turned her head. The peonies sat on the bedside table, their petals a stark spill of white against the sterile hospital grays.

A quiet noise escaped Penn's throat—some hybrid of a sigh and a laugh. His head tilted back against the pillow. "You brought me flowers."

"Yeah," Victoria said, matching her sister as she too flushed. "I realized when I was picking them out that I don't actually know your favorite flower, so I went with mine. Was it selfish? Yes. Was I too stressed to care? Also yes."

He smiled. "I love them."

"Are they your favorite?" Clara asked.

Penn gave Victoria an awkward smile. "Not exactly. But they're beautiful too."

Clara wrinkled her nose. "Well, are you going to tell us what your favorite flower is? Or are you going to make us guess?"

"Guessing would be fun. But no, my favorite flowers have been the Vanessa Bell rose for a very long time." Penn met Victoria's gaze and held it as he spoke.

Clara groaned, rolling her eyes so hard her whole head lolled back. "Oh my god. You would have a favorite flower with the same name as her. That's disgusting." She mimed gagging. "I'm gonna hurl."

Victoria ignored her sister and squeezed his hand. "I love you," she said, the words tumbling out before she could second-guess them.

Penn grinned, and his fingers tightened around hers. "Yeah?"

"Yeah."

"I guess it's a good thing I love you too."

Clara groaned louder, clapping her hands over her ears. "Nope. I'm out. Done. You two are gross."

"You'll be gross someday too. Maybe. If you can get anyone to see past your agonizing flaws," Victoria said, sticking her tongue out at her sister. Clara returned the gesture.

The hospital room door creaked open, and Victoria lifted her gaze as Carson stepped in. Behind him, a woman with dark curly hair lingered, her fingers brushing the sleeve of his jacket.

"Hey Cars," Penn greeted with a nod. "Kinsley, this is Victoria and her sister Clara."

The woman glanced at Victoria, her smile warm. "Hi. I'm Kinsley, Carson's fiancée."

"Hi." Victoria extended a hand. Kinsley's grip was firm, her fingers cold. She had the kind of presence that was both approachable and guarded, like she was used to being watched. Victoria could relate.

Before Kinsley could say more, the door swung open again, and Benedict slipped in with yet another woman at his side. Dark hair framed her freckled face, and her dark eyes darted around the room. She was carrying a paper bag in one hand and a bouquet of lilies in the other.

"Hey, everyone," the woman said, her voice loud and warm. "Sorry we're late. Benedict here decided we needed to stop for snacks."

Carson rolled his eyes, then nodded towards the woman. "My little sister, Paisley. And yes, she is dating Benedict."

"We're engaged too, asshole," Paisley said, flipping her brother off. "Whether you like it or not.'

"Uh huh," Carson muttered, pinching the bridge of his nose. "Pai, this is Victoria and Clara."

Again, Victoria smiled and shook a stranger's hand. "It's nice to meet you."

Clara perked up at the mention of food. "What kind of snacks did you bring?"

"Everything," Paisley said, dumping the contents of the bag onto the small table by the bed. Chips, candy bars, and a few wrapped sandwiches spilled out. "Help yourself."

Clara didn't need to be told twice. She grabbed a candy bar and leaned back in her chair, peeling the wrapper.

"How are you doing, Penn?" Benedict asked.

"I'll live. I think. Right?" He glanced at Victoria, who nodded.

"Yeah, I'll live. And I might get a cool scar. Speaking of scars, where's Tanner?" Penn asked, glancing toward the door.

As if on cue, Tanner strode in, his towering frame filling the doorway. Yet another woman followed close behind, her hair pulled back in a sleek chignon.

"Omstadt, little Omstadt, this is my wife," Tanner said with a quick nod towards the woman.

"I do have a name, dickhead."

"Uh huh," he mumbled, shrugging and moving to lean against the opposite wall.

She rolled her eyes and stepped forward, her hand extended. "Excuse him. We're still working on manners. I'm Blair. And you must be Victoria."

Victoria shook her hand. "Nice to meet you, Blair. That's my sister, Clara."

Clara, mouth full of chocolate, gave a half-hearted wave.

"Obviously, we're still working on manners too," Victoria said, rolling her eyes. Blair chuckled and went to stand next to Tanner. He was over a head taller than her, and the height difference was almost comical.

The door opened once more, and finally it was a woman Victoria recognized. Jenna slipped in, her auburn hair in its usual braid. James was right behind her, his broad shoulders nearly brushing the doorframe. He was slightly flushed in the face as he glanced around the room and gave a small nod in greeting.

"Looks like we're all here," Jenna said, scanning the group. "How's the patient?"

"As I said before, I'm alive," Penn said again. "Clara's making sure I stay that way."

Clara smirked. "Somebody has to."

Paisley slung her arm around Benedict's waist, surveying the cramped room with a raised brow. "Pretty sure there's a max occupancy for these places. Are we going to get kicked out?"

Carson pulled his phone from his pocket, scrolling idly. "Made a sizable donation to the hospital. We're good for another forty-five minutes."

Kinsley snorted, elbowing him. "Of course you did."

"What? It's efficient."

Clara wrinkled her nose, scrunching her candy wrapper into a ball. "Don't worry, I'll give you all some space." She shoved out of her chair, stretching her arms overhead. "I'm gonna go find a computer."

"Take Jenna with you," Victoria said automatically.

"Nope." Clara pointed at her sister. "Problems gone. Besides, you're insufferable when you're in worry-mode." She winked and ducked out before anyone could argue.

James whistled low, rubbing the back of his neck. "Kid's got attitude."

"And trauma," Victoria muttered, half to herself.

Penn laced his fingers through hers, thumb tracing slow circles over her knuckles. The heart monitor beeped steadily in the background as the room lapsed into easy silence—well, as easy as it could be with ten personalities crammed into one space.

Tanner rolled his shoulders, stretching. "For the record, if you ever pull that self-sacrificial crap again, Levine, I'll put you back in the hospital myself."

Blair smacked his bicep. "He almost bled out. Read the room."

"Yeah, yeah."

Penn smirked. "I'm touched to know you care, Whitney."

"Eh, fuck you."

"Fuck you back," Penn flipped him off with a grin on his face, which Tanner returned in kind.

Jenna rolled her eyes. "You were already passing out when we got there. We were almost too late."

Victoria's grip on Penn's hand tightened. The memory of him slumped against the cellar floor, blood soaking through his shirt, flashed behind her eyelids. She forced a breath. "I don't think I ever thanked you. All of you."

Benedict tipped his head. "Anytime."

"Jesus, this is getting sentimental," Carson muttered, rubbing his temple. "I was shot too."

Paisley elbowed her brother hard. "Don't be an asshole."

"Join the club," Tanner muttered.

"Which club? The asshole club or I-survived-getting-shot club?" Jenna asked.

Tanner gave her a once over and then shrugged with a deadpan face. "You fit both, Briggs."

James snorted, and Jenna glared at him. "What? He's right."

Penn let out a low chuckle, wincing almost immediately. Victoria shot him a look, and he mouthed, *I'm fine*, before glancing around the room. "So, uh. Since we're all here, how did you guys get me out?"

Jenna and Tanner exchanged a look.

"We waited for a signal, and after we didn't get one, we breached," Tanner said, like that explained everything.

Jenna snorted. "Translation: Tanner kicked the door in."

"It was locked."

Blair sighed. "Men."

Penn sagged back into his pillow, grinning. "Glad to know my survival came down to Tanner's shoe."

Tanner gave a half-shrug. "Worked, didn't it?"

Victoria exhaled, shaking her head. "I couldn't give a signal. As soon as he got me to the house, he checked and found the comms device. Ripped it right off me."

Penn squeezed her hand. "You okay?"

She swallowed past the tightness in her throat. "Yeah."

He didn't look convinced, but he let it go, turning back to the others. "So, what'd I miss? World still standing?"

Benedict groaned. "Ugh, don't ask. Cars pissed off another senator yesterday."

"He had it coming," Carson said, completely unrepentant.

The conversation spiraled from there—work, politics, Tanner's latest near-death experience (according to Blair). Victoria leaned against the bed railing, watching Penn's face as he followed the banter, his thumb still brushing absently over her fingers. God, he really did love them, and they loved him. It was more than she could've ever wished for that scrawny high school boy.

He caught her staring. "What?"

She shook her head. "Nothing. I'm just glad you found me."

"Even if I stalked you for four years?" Penn asked, eyebrow raised.

"Even then."

Penn flashed her a grin, and then flipped off every man in that room. "She's happy I stalked her, so suck it boys. It really does work."

EPILOGUE
PENN

THE LIGHTS DIMMED, PLUNGING THE THEATER INTO darkness. Penn tucked his hands into his pockets, leaning back against the plush velvet seat—same one he'd reserved for four years running. Except now, instead of watching from the shadows, Clara sat beside him, kicking her legs impatiently.

"You okay?" Penn muttered, glancing at her.

She rolled her eyes. "You asked me that, like, five times."

The orchestra swelled, and the stage lit up in a wash of gold. Victoria—his Victoria—stepped into the spotlight. The crowd erupted into applause.

And Penn? He stopped breathing.

She wasn't just in the ensemble anymore. This was her show now. Her name on the playbill, her voice carrying across the theater, owning every damn second of it. And when she turned in their direction mid-performance—*his* direction—she paused, just for a fraction of a second. He doubted she could see him, but she knew he was there.

Clara elbowed him. Hard.

"Stop swooning. You're embarrassing me," she whispered.

"Stop talking, you're ruining the show," he whispered back.

They both remained silent for the rest of the performance.

And after the show, he brought Clara backstage. It was chaos, but Penn knew the exact path to Victoria's personal dressing room. He could've navigated it in his sleep—had, once, during a nightmare that sent him to check on her at 3 AM. (She'd been fine. He'd gotten a pillow thrown at his head for waking her.)

Clara trailed behind him. "Can we hurry? I want food."

Penn ignored her. He'd brought white peonies, same as always. Except now, instead of signing them with a fake name, he pressed a kiss to Victoria's cheek before handing them over every time.

"You came!" Victoria grinned, still buzzing from the high of the performance. Then she caught sight of Clara and blinked. "Wait—you're here?"

Clara shrugged, plopping onto the couch and snagging a bottle of water. "Summer break. Nothing better to do."

Penn shot her a look.

"What? I was bored," Clara muttered.

Victoria shook her head, laughing. "Uh-huh, sure." She turned to Penn, studying him like she was reading his mind. "How bad was it? I know I missed a few of the high notes, and I nearly forgot one of my lines in the second act, but—"

Penn grabbed her around the waist and kissed her, trying to ignore the cloying scent of hairspray that radiated off her. "You were perfect," he whispered against her lips. "Fucking perfect."

"Does that mean I get a reward?" Victoria whispered back, trailing her lips along his jaw as she wrapped her arms around his neck. God, she was gorgeous, even covered in fifty pounds of stage makeup.

"Absolutely."

Clara made a gagging noise. "Okay, gross. Are we getting dinner or what?"

Victoria chuckled and reluctantly let go of Penn. "Patience is not your virtue."

"Never claimed it was," Clara shot back.

———

THE PENTHOUSE SMELLED LIKE PEPPERONI AND GARLIC, the coffee table cluttered with empty soda cans and three open pizza boxes—two half-eaten, one entirely demolished by Clara. Sandy sprawled across their laps, a warm, pleased lump, grunting softly whenever someone shifted too much.

Penn barely noticed the controller in his hands. He was too busy stealing glances at Victoria.

She sat cross-legged beside him, the sleeves of Penn's old MIT hoodie rolled up past her wrists, hair piled messily on top of her head. She scowled at the screen, tongue poking between her teeth in concentration as her character dodged another attack.

"Clara, you little cheat," Victoria huffed.

Clara didn't even look up, fingers flying over the controller. "Not cheating. Just better."

Penn's character ragdolled off-screen, and the game blared *DEFEAT* in bold red letters.

"Bullshit," he muttered.

Clara smirked. "That's, what, five rounds straight?"

Victoria groaned, tossing her controller onto the couch. "I used to be good at this."

"Aw, sweet sister, you were never good at this," Clara said sweetly.

Penn watched them, the way Victoria shoved at Clara's shoulder, how Clara leaned into the touch instead of flinching away like she had in those first few weeks after Morrison. The bruises on her arms were long faded, but the way she startled at sudden movements still made Penn's muscles tighten.

Not anymore, though. Tonight, Clara was just a kid. A loud, obnoxious, infuriatingly talented kid—who he maybe, kind of, had let win a few times to see that smug grin.

Victoria twisted toward him, poking his ribs. "You're supposed to be a tech genius. Can't you hack the game?"

"Tempting." He caught her finger before she could retreat, lacing their hands together just because he could.

Sandy let out a grumbling sigh, adjusting between them.

Clara snorted, already resetting the match. "You guys are gross."

"And yet," Victoria mused, "somehow, you're the one who keeps crashing on our couch."

"Please." Clara rolled her eyes. "Your guest room has better Wi-Fi than Mom's place."

"My guest room has better Wi-Fi than 90% of the city." Penn bragged as he downed the rest of his energy drink.

The TV flickered as the next round loaded, casting blue reflections across Victoria's face.

This—this was what he'd wanted, back when he'd watched her from a distance. This warmth. The messy domesticity of takeout and gaming and Victoria's socked foot nudging against his thigh. She fit here, in his space, like she'd always been part of it.

Clara's eyes darted between them. "Oh my god, you're doing the thing again."

"What thing?" Penn asked.

"The gross staring thing." She waved a hand between them. "Like you're both thinking about kissing. Or worse."

Victoria choked on her soda. "Clara," she warned, her teeth pressed together so it came out more threatening. "Watch it."

Penn grabbed the controller. "Let's do a rematch."

"Fine." Clara grinned. "But I'm still gonna win."

And she did. Only because Penn let her, but he wasn't going to tell either woman that. It was too satisfying to see the glee on Clara's face, and in turn, the contented expression hidden beneath a playful pout on Victoria's lips.

Penn stretched, arm settling along the back of the couch behind Victoria. "Rigged game."

"Sore loser." Clara set the controller down and flopped back against the cushions.

Victoria curled into his side, breath soft against his collarbone. "Yeah," she murmured, voice low enough that only he could hear. "Total sore loser."

Her fingers skimmed his waist, and she leaned towards him, kissing along his jaw.

Clara made a disgusted noise and grabbed Sandy, burying her face in fur. "I'm taking the dog to the guest room to sleep. Wake me up when you two are done being gross."

Penn flicked a pizza crust at her.

She flicked it back.

And Victoria just laughed—a sound he'd spent years listening to through covert surveillance, one that belonged to him now, no encryption needed.

———

THE MOMENT PENN HEARD THE BIOMETRIC LOCK CHIME, his fingers stilled over the keyboard. The only people with access were Carson, the other guys, and Victoria. He swiveled in his chair just as Victoria stepped through the door, and his jaw nearly unhinged.

She wore one of his old MIT hoodies—threadbare, hanging off one shoulder—and nothing else but those little lace shorts that made his brain short-circuit. Her hair was piled high, loose strands framing her flushed cheeks. But it was the mischievous twist of her mouth that set his pulse galloping.

"You're supposed to be taking Clara to the airport," he blurted.

"Babe, that was eight hours ago." She kicked the door shut, readjusting the bag on her shoulder. "You've been hiding away for a lifetime, and I missed you."

Penn swallowed. His monitors reflected Victoria's slow prowl through the maze of servers, her fingertips tracing cables. Her hips swayed just enough to hold his attention hostage.

His chair squeaked as he stood. "Did you need help with something?"

"Thought that was obvious." She stopped beside his primary workstation, where a half-finished algorithm blinked across three screens. Then she reached into her bag and pulled out a sleek black case.

Penn's brain shorted out when she snapped it open, revealing the unmistakable shape of her pink vibrator—the one he'd accidentally found in her bathroom, the one he'd thought about more times than he'd admit. There were other toys he hadn't seen before in the bag too.

Jesus Christ.

Victoria tilted her head, feigning innocence. "We've been on best behavior for Clara."

"Yeah." His voice cracked. "We have."

"And I'm tired of being good." She tilted her head, smirking at him. "I've been thinking about your lab. About you, all alone in here. Thought you might like some company."

Fuck. His throat went dry. He had, in fact, imagined her sprawled across his desk, surrounded by the hum of servers, backlit by the glow of his monitors. But reality was better, because she was the one pushing him toward his desk now, palms planted on his chest until the edge hit his ass.

"You ever fuck someone in here?" She leaned into him and traced the shell of his ear with her teeth.

No, because no one else *would be stupid enough to let me.* "No."

"Good." Her hand slipped between them, palming him through his jeans. "Then I get to be first, right?"

"Hell yeah."

"Good boy."

She made quick work of his clothes, her touch slow in some places, impatient in others. Penn barely registered his shirt hitting the floor before Victoria was on her knees, mouthing along his hipbone while she worked open his fly.

Penn's breath hitched as Victoria's fingers curled into the waistband of his briefs, dragging them down just enough to expose him. Her gaze flicked up—green eyes dark with amusement—as she traced the length of him with her tongue. A slow, teasing press against the underside from base to tip, pausing to swirl at the head until he groaned.

"Fuck, Ness." His fingers flexed against the edge of his desk, knuckles white. He pressed his glasses farther up the bridge of his nose, not wanting to miss a detail.

She hummed, the vibration making his hips jerk. "I love that you still call me that," she murmured, before taking him into her mouth. Not all at once. Not how he wanted. Her lips barely covered the crown, her tongue working circles until his thighs trembled. Then deeper, inch by torturous inch, until her nose brushed his pelvis.

Penn's head tipped back, his exhale ragged. He forced himself to keep his hands off her. But fuck, he wanted to twist his fingers in her hair and fuck her mouth until she choked. The surrounding servers hummed, the monitors casting shifting blue light over her bare shoulder where his hoodie had slipped.

Just as his muscles coiled, pleasure tightening at the base of his spine, Victoria pulled back, letting him slip free with a wet sound. Cool air hit him, and he choked on a curse.

Her grin was wicked as she wiped her mouth with the back of her hand. "Almost got you."

His laugh was breathless. "You're a menace."

She pressed a kiss to the inside of his thigh, just above where the fabric of his briefs still clung. "Yes, yes I am."

Victoria ducked back down, this time taking him deep without warning. She hollowed her cheeks, the suction perfect, her rhythm relentless. One hand worked the base, twisting in time with each pull of her mouth. The other slid behind her own neck, gathering her hair, giving him an unobstructed view of every movement—the way her lips stretched, the flutter of her lashes when he twitched against her tongue.

Penn bit out an incoherent noise, hips jerking forward. "Close—"

Again, she pulled back, her breath warm against his spit-slick skin. "Nope."

"Fuck," he ground out, dragging a hand through his own hair. His pulse hammered under his skin, the ache almost painful.

Victoria nipped his hipbone, her fingers toying with the elastic of his briefs. "You watched me for years, and now I finally get to watch you?" She pressed an open-mouthed kiss just below his navel, her exhale fanning across his skin as she murmured, "Payback's a bitch, isn't it?"

Then she swallowed him whole.

This time, her rhythm was punishing—no teasing, just relentless suction, her throat fluttering around him when he hit the back of it. She gagged, but kept going. Winding him higher and higher and higher. One of his hands finally caved, tangling in her hair, not guiding, just holding, grounding himself. The desk groaned under his grip with his other hand, screws straining.

He was right there, pleasure sparking up his spine, when—

She stopped.

"No, no, fuck—"

Victoria rocked back on her heels, licking her lips. She didn't even look winded. "Tell me," she said, palming him again, loose and slow just to watch his hips buck. "How many times did you watch me touch myself on your cameras?"

"I didn't. Always cut off before." He groaned, heat crawling up his neck—Victoria in dim lamplight, hand between her thighs, gasping into her pillow. And that damn vibrator nearing her clit. "But fuck, I wish I had."

She laughed, breathless. "That's what I thought." Then, just as his cock jumped in her grip, she leaned in, mouth brushing the tip of his dick. "How would you like to play with my toys?"

His hands were on her before she finished speaking, dragging her up by the waist, his mouth crashing into hers. She gasped into the kiss as he yanked the hoodie over her head in one smooth motion, tossing it onto a buzzing server stack. The bralette followed—just a scrap of lace that barely covered anything anyway—bouncing off a monitor.

His fingers dug into her hips as he lifted her onto the nearest desk, scattering a pile of hard drives. The clatter made Victoria laugh, but he swallowed the sound, kissing her like he could fucking consume her. She arched into him, bare skin against his chest, her nails raking down his back.

Penn pulled back just far enough to reach into the bag beside her, knocking it over. An avalanche of sex toys spilled out—vibrators, a slender dildo, a set of chrome-plated cuffs, and—*oh shit*—a blindfold with an absurd lace trim that made his pulse hammer harder. But what really got him was the tiny remote control, no bigger than a poker chip.

"What's this?"

Victoria gave a little shrug and nodded towards it. "Not sure. Why don't you figure it out?"

He reached for it, turning the small device over in his hand. There was an on-and-off switch and a plus and minus button. That was it. He traced his thumb over the plus button before clicking it once.

Victoria bit her lip, shifting just enough for him to catch the faintest hum beneath the lace of her shorts.

Jesus. Christ.

His gaze snapped to her. "You've got to be fucking kidding me."

Penn's grip on her thigh tightened as he thumbed the remote, flicking the dial up again without warning. Victoria jolted, a sharp gasp tearing from her throat as the vibration buzzed against her clit. He watched, hypnotized, as her fingers scrabbled against the desk, her hips rolling instinctively.

"Had it in the whole time?" His voice was rough, fingers ghosting over the waistband of her shorts.

She nodded, breathless. "From the moment I walked in."

His groan was pure, unfiltered want. He cranked the remote higher, watching her legs tremble, the flush creeping down her chest. "And the others?"

A shaky exhale. "Wanted you to... oh *fuck*—pick."

Penn dragged the shorts down just enough to expose the vibrator nestled against her. He replaced it with his thumb, pressing firm circles while his other hand dug through the pile of toys. The glass dildo was cold in his palm, condensation already forming as he passed it between his fingers.

"On your back," he ordered, nudging her shoulders until she lay against the desk. He pulled her shorts all the way off, sending them and the vibrator flying behind him.

Victoria didn't hesitate. She hooked her legs over his shoulders, and Penn nearly lost his goddamn mind at the sight—her thighs wet already. He curved the glass toy against her, dragging it up her slick slit before circling her entrance, just teasing, just testing.

"Penn—"

"Tell me," he murmured, pressing the tip against her, watching her muscles flutter. "Which one of these have you thought about me using on you?"

Her laugh was shaky. "All of them."

Fuck. Fuck.

He pushed the dildo in slow, the glass warming instantly as her body swallowed it. Victoria arched off the desk, cursing, her hands scrambling for purchase.

Penn watched the glass dildo disappear into Victoria inch by inch, her hips lifting off the desk to meet him. He twisted it slightly, dragging the curved tip along her inner walls just to hear her moan.

God, the noises she made.

He curled his fingers around the pink vibrator, thumbing it on to the lowest setting before bringing it to her clit. The second it touched her, Victoria jerked, her hand flying to clutch his wrist. "Fuck—"

"I thought you wanted me to play with your toys." He swirled the vibrator in tight circles, watching her back arch, her nails dig into his skin.

She exhaled a broken laugh. "Fuck, Penn, yes."

He didn't ease up. Kept the dildo moving inside her, angling it just so every time he pulled it back, then pressing the vibrator harder against her.

Victoria's breath came in short gasps now, her lashes fluttering, lips parted. Penn drank in every flicker of pleasure on her face—the twitch of her brow when he hit a particular spot, the way she bit down on her lower lip to stifle a sound.

He didn't want her quiet.

"Remember how you didn't let me come?" He twisted the dildo deeper.

A ragged moan tore out of her. The desk creaked under her shifting weight, the metal legs screeching against the concrete floor. Penn didn't care. He was too focused on the way her body tightened around the glass, the way her clit pulsed under the insistent buzz of the vibrator.

"I'm nicer than you, I guess, because I'm going to let you come. In fact, you're going to finish over and over until I get bored of your toys."

"Penn," she gasped. "I'm—"

"I know." He could feel it—the way her muscles fluttered, the shiver running through her. He pressed the vibrator firmer, holding it steady as he fucked her with the dildo, watching, waiting—

Victoria came with a choked cry, back bowing off the desk. Her eyelids slammed shut, her thighs clamping around his wrist as she shuddered. Penn kept the pace unrelenting, drawing it out, until her fingers scrabbled at his arm.

"Too—*too much*—"

He pulled the vibrator away, but left the dildo buried inside her, letting her ride out the aftershocks. She collapsed back onto the desk, chest heaving, hair a wild tangle around her shoulders. Her skin was flushed, sweat glistening along her collarbone.

Penn dragged the glass toy out slowly, watching her breath catch at the sensation. He moved it aside with a clatter, then leaned down, bracing his hands on either side of her head.

"Ready for the next toy?"

Victoria blinked up at him, dazed. "I... yeah."

Penn's fingers trailed lightly up Victoria's inner thighs, relishing the tremor that followed his touch. "Turn around," he murmured tapping her on the hip.

She obeyed without hesitation, shifting on the desk until she faced away from him. Penn palmed her ass before retrieving the chrome handcuffs from the scattered pile of toys.

"These okay?" He kissed the curve of her shoulder, waiting for her nod before clicking the first cuff around her wrist.

Victoria exhaled sharply when the cold metal touched her skin, but arched back into him, her wet pussy grinding against his dick, as he secured her other hand behind her. Penn made sure they weren't too tight—just enough restraint to tease, not hurt.

He reached for the blindfold next, smoothing his fingers along the lace trim before brushing her hair aside to secure it. Victoria shuddered when the soft fabric blocked her vision, her breath stuttering as Penn traced the curve of her spine with his tongue.

"So good," he murmured.

She laughed breathlessly, rocking her hips back against him. "I aim to please."

Penn hummed, slipping two fingers through her slick folds—still wet from her last orgasm—before dragging up, circling her tight, asshole. Victoria tensed instinctively, exhaling sharply as he teased.

"Relax," Penn murmured, coating his fingers in her own wetness before pressing one inside—slowly, carefully. She gasped, muscles fluttering around him. "How often have you used the plug?"

"Once or t-twice," she stuttered, her breath catching as he pressed his finger in farther.

"Is this okay?" He rested his free hand on her lower back, steadying her as she adjusted.

Victoria nodded, hair tumbling to one side as she pressed her cheek into the desk. "Yeah—just... different."

Penn worked his finger deeper, twisting gently, relishing the soft noises spilling from her lips. Every time he pulled out far enough, he spat on his finger, making sure it slipped easily in and out. He added a second finger gradually, stretching her until she rocked back onto his hand with a choked moan.

"Look at you," Penn breathed, sliding his fingers free just long enough to retrieve the sleek black plug. A small bottle of lube had fallen out among the toys, and he grabbed it, covering the black silicone until it glistened. He pressed the tapered tip into her entrance, groaning when she arched into it.

Her breath came in shallow pants as he pushed it in—inch by careful inch—until the flared base settled snugly against her. Penn ghosted his fingers along the seams of her thighs, admiring how full she looked, how perfectly she took it.

"Fuck—" Victoria twisted her wrists in the cuffs, her cheek pressing into the desk.

Penn smirked and flipped the switch on the base of the plug. It buzzed to life with a soft hum.

"Penn!"

He chuckled, gripping her hips as she jolted, thighs trembling. "Hold still."

She pressed her forehead against the desk, helpless laughter mixing with moans as Penn lined himself up, dragging his cock through her slick folds before sinking into her in one smooth slow thrust.

Penn's hands tightened on Victoria's hips as he pushed into her, her slick heat swallowing him whole. The desk groaned beneath them, monitors flickering with abandoned code as she arched back into his thrusts. The faint buzz of the plug travelled through her inner walls, a phantom vibration against his dick that made his pulse spike.

"Are you breathing?" His fingers skimmed up her spine to twist in her hair gently, just enough to tilt her head back.

Victoria's laugh dissolved into a moan as he rocked deeper, her cuffed wrists straining. "Barely. That thing's... fuck, Penn—"

He pressed the button on the plug, cranking the vibration higher. Her body clenched around him like a vice, forcing a ragged groan from his throat. Christ, she was tight.

Penn's fingers trailed up Victoria's spine as he pulled out slowly, relishing the way her breath hitched. The plug buzzed faintly inside her, making her clench around nothing, and he smirked at the shudder that racked her body.

"You're too quiet," he murmured, gripping her hips and yanking her back against him in one sharp thrust.

Victoria gasped, her forehead pressing into the desk, her fingers flexing uselessly against the cuffs. "Fuck!" She shrieked.

"Yeah, that's better." Penn dragged his palm over her ass before bringing it down in a sharp smack. The sound cracked through the lab, echoing off the monitors.

Her hips bucked forward instinctively before rocking back against him. "Again."

Penn obliged, landing another slap, harder this time, watching the

138

flush bloom across her skin. He mapped the heat with his fingertips before spreading her cheeks wider, his cock sliding deeper with each rough thrust.

Victoria whined, shifting her weight and forcing her ass higher. "More."

Penn chuckled darkly, reaching around to pinch her clit between his thumb and forefinger. He twisted sharply, just once, and she jerked against him with a choked-off cry.

Her thighs trembled, sweat glistening along her taut muscles as the plug's vibrations echoed through her. Penn leaned forward, increasing the vibrations once more as his thrusts turned punishing, the slap of skin filling the space between the hum of servers.

"I—" Victoria's voice fragmented, her spine bowing as pleasure coiled tighter. "Penn, I'm gonna—"

"Do it," he ordered and rubbed her clit. "Now."

She shattered with a ragged scream, her entire body locking up before collapsing against the desk, trembling uncontrollably. Penn didn't stop, fucking her through it, chasing his own release behind clenched teeth.

The blindfold slipped as she turned her head toward him, lips parted, chest heaving. "Penn—"

That was all it took—just his name—and he came with a ragged groan, burying himself inside her until his release filled her.

The monitors cast a flickering blue light across Victoria's bare skin as she lay sprawled across his desk, still catching her breath. He flipped the plug off and removed her blindfold, grinning at her. She smiled back, letting out a contented sigh.

"You did so well," he said, tracing the curve of her hip where the handcuffs had left faint marks, his fingers gliding over sweat-damp skin. She shivered when his touch grazed the plug still nested inside her.

Victoria turned her head, her cheek pressed to the polished steel surface of his workstation. "You going to free my wrists?"

Penn snorted, dragging a thumb over her wrist. "Maybe."

"Maybe?" She arched an eyebrow. "Are you thinking there's more?"

Shrugging, he reached for the plug and flicked it back on—low, just enough to make her jolt. Victoria's breath hitched, her thighs pressing together instinctively.

"I did say you'd come over and over, and over again. And we did behave while your sister was here."

Her glare lacked heat. "Asshole."

Penn smirked, smacking her ass cheek enough to make her jump. He rubbed the faint red marks left behind. "Yes, that's exactly where the toy is. Good job."

"One of these days, it's going in your asshole. Then we'll see how much you like it."

He turned the intensity higher, and she swore. "Challenge accepted."

READ THE FIRST CHAPTER IN THE
NEXT NOVELLA IN THE BILLIONAIRES
OF CREST STRATEGIES SERIES

A DARK BILLIONAIRE ROMANCE NOVELLA

WRECKED
Fates

ELORA RAE

CHAPTER 1
JENNA

"I said harder, damn it," Jenna hissed. The fluorescent light flickered through the slats in the utility closet door, striping James's broad shoulders as he drove into her. Jenna dug her fingers into his biceps. His muscles flexed under her grip with each punishing thrust. His forearm braced under her knee, keeping her leg hooked over him, the angle ruthless and perfect.

"That—fuck, right there—" she gasped into the junction of his neck and shoulder, teeth scraping skin.

A low growl rumbled in James' chest. His free hand clamped over her hip, hauling her harder onto him. The edge of a metal shelf bit into her back.

She raked her nails down his spine. "Again."

He obeyed instantly—no teasing, no hesitation. He knew exactly how to wreck her. The sound of skin slapping skin mingled with their ragged breaths. Jenna tilted her head back as the coil in her belly tightened to breaking.

James' mouth found her throat. "Gonna come?"

She reached behind her blindly, gripping the shelf above, swallowing a curse as the pressure splintered inside her. "Do that thing with your thumb."

His laugh was dark, but his thumb swiped over her clit anyway, rough and just slightly too hard—exactly how she liked it. She shattered, biting down on his trapezius to muffle the scream clawing its way up her throat. James followed with a stifled groan, his hips jerking erratically before he stilled, forehead pressed against the wall beside her head.

The only sounds were their panting breaths. Then James stepped back, yanking his slacks up and offered her a handkerchief. The embroidered JWR in the corner was still crisp—military neat even when used to wipe off a woman's thighs.

Jenna cleaned herself in quick swipes, ignoring the way her pulse still rabbited under her skin. "We need to go."

James adjusted his cuffs, the picture of composed indifference aside from the faint flush still high on his cheeks. "Penn's stable. Another five minutes wouldn't have mattered."

"Spoken like a man who wasn't the one bleeding out on a fucking gurney two days ago." She yanked her underwear up and reached for her blouse, buttoning it. Two years of this—airports, alleyways, the occasional safe-house cot—and they'd gotten it down to a science. No cuddling. No whispered promises. Just hard, hungry friction and an exit strategy.

James snagged his tie from a shelf of IV bags. "I'm sure the rest of them are keeping him busy."

Jenna shoved her hair back into its braid. "I'm sure Carson is already trying to find a way to get the attention on him."

The corner of James' mouth ticked up. "Definitely."

She palmed the door handle. "And, Rothschild?"

His gray eyes flicked to hers.

"You should've bought me dinner first." The joke tasted smooth as always.

He smirked, straightening his collar. "I'll remember that for next time, Briggs."

"You better." She pushed the door open to the sterile hospital glare, stepping into the hall without looking back.

The walls went up. They always did.

Inside Penn's hospital room, Crest Strategies had taken over entirely—Paisley perched on the foot of Penn's bed chattering animatedly, Carson leaning against the windowsill with his usual intensity, Kinsley at his side, Blair scowling at something Tanner muttered under his breath. Victoria stood directly next to the bed, her hand in Penn's. Benedict lingered near the wall, gaze flicking between everyone.

They'd been there for a while, Jenna and James having arrived last. The conversation had gone back and forth, and no one seemed to have noticed that the two of them had arrived together. No one, except fucking Tanner Whitney. The ass.

"So, it took you two long enough to get here," Tanner rumbled, thick arms crossed over his chest. His wife, Blair, glanced up at him with a warning look in her eyes, but she didn't say anything.

James pulled up a chair beside Penn's bed. "Had phone calls."

"Checking in with one of my teams," Jenna said at the same time.

Penn's eyebrows twitched. Tanner's lips curled into something far too smug.

Carson barely glanced up from his phone. "If you're done interrogating them like a jealous husband, Tanner, we've got a rogue PR firestorm brewing with that governor. Can you do damage control?"

Penn leaned forward—too fast—wincing as his IV tugged.

James shot him a look. "Easy. He asked Tanner, not you."

"Yeah, well, I want to help." Penn muttered, adjusting the bandages peeking from beneath his hospital gown. "Unfortunately, not all of us bounce back like you military freaks."

Jenna snorted. "Should've stayed behind your screens."

Penn flipped her off.

Apparently, Tanner wasn't done. He tilted his head toward James. "Phone calls, huh?"

James didn't react, rolling his shoulders as if he couldn't be bothered. "Yeah, and? It's part of my job, Whitney."

Penn tilted his head suddenly, squinting. "James."

James glanced at him. "What?"

Penn grinned. "Your collar's crooked."

A beat. James flicked it back into place too late.

Penn's grin widened. "And you've got a bruise."

Silence.

Blair's gaze flicked over. Benedict coughed into his fist. Paisley choked on her water.

James exhaled sharply, dragging a hand through his hair. "I relieve stress how I want." His gaze pinned Carson, Tanner, and Penn in turn. "Especially when my friends keep jumping in front of bullets."

Carson rolled his eyes. Tanner barked a laugh. Penn grinned wider.

"You're welcome," Penn said sweetly.

The tension dissolved. Mostly. Jenna leaned against the far wall, arms crossed, ignoring the weight of James' gaze when it slid her way a second too long. He was usually good at hiding things. Usually. Apparently, today was not one of those days.

Jenna left twenty minutes later, claiming fatigue, which wasn't entirely a lie. He really had tired her out in that closet.

The hospital parking lot was quiet, the cold bite of midnight air grounding against her overheated skin. Jenna slid into her SUV, gripping the wheel.

This is fine.

She exhaled through her nose.

This is manageable.

She rolled her neck in circles a few times.

This was just for stress relief.

Her phone buzzed against the console. She snatched it up and smirked when she saw James's name on the screen.

Mine. 20 minutes.

This won't totally wreck me.

She fired a confirmation text back before tossing her phone aside. And if her foot pressed harder on the accelerator than necessary—well. No one had to know.

READ THE REST OF JAMES AND
JENNA'S STORY IN THE NEXT
BILLIONAIRES OF CREST STRATEGIES
NOVELLA:

WRECKED
Fates

MAKE SURE TO CHECK OUT
ALL FIVE BOOKS IN THE
BILLIONAIRES OF CREST STRATEGIES SERIES

ACKNOWLEDGMENTS

I somehow published another book. If you're reading this, it means *Coded Truths* has joined his three older brothers. I definitely think this one is the cutest out of all of my stalk-y, murderer-y, dark romance books in this series. It was kind of refreshing to have Penn as an MMC after the terrifying Tanner Whitney in book three..

First, thank you to my parents, who are supportive as always. I appreciate the not-so-quiet concern about my browser history. Valid, honestly.

To my brother, who gives unwavering support without understanding a damn thing about what I do is exactly the kind of blind loyalty Penn would appreciate.

To my beta readers: Dani R., Mariah S., Rachel H., and Zoe M. - thank you for not calling the authorities when you read Penn's surveillance protocols. Your feedback helped me walk the line between "romantic obsession" and "restraining order territory."

Writing *Coded Truths* was like trying to make stalking romantic while also making it believable (as if having a multi-million dollar tech lab is a normal thing). Publishing it feels like confessing my own questionable fantasies and hoping you share them. Thank you for trusting me with your most unhinged book boyfriend desires.

Thank you for reading, for understanding that sometimes love looks like cameras and flowers, and for not judging me too harshly for making the stalker the good guy.

Stay beautifully unhinged, Elora Rae

P.S. Also, Penn is watching you. He'll know if you don't leave a rating and a review…

ABOUT THE AUTHOR

Elora Rae is a longtime lover of dark romance, drawn to stories about morally grey men, obsessive love, and twisted secrets. When she's not writing, Elora is probably re-reading her favorite villain origin love stories or plotting the next emotionally delicious downfall. These books are just the beginning.

www.ingramcontent.com/pod-product-compliance
Lightning Source LLC
Chambersburg PA
CBHW020417150626
46554CB00014B/1884